Blanche McCrary Boyd
May 16, 1991

Also by Blanche McCrary Boyd

NERVES

MOURNING THE DEATH OF MAGIC

THE REDNECK WAY OF KNOWLEDGE

The Revolution of Little Girls

THE
REVOLUTION
of Little Girls

BLANCHE
McCRARY
BOYD

ALFRED A. KNOPF NEW YORK 1991

This Is a Borzoi Book
Published by Alfred A. Knopf, Inc.

Copyright © 1991 by Blanche McCrary Boyd

Portions of this work were originally published, in somewhat different form, in the *VLS (Voice Literary Supplement)* and *Special Report.*

Grateful acknowledgment is made to the following for permission to reprint previously published material:
Ice Nine Publishing Company, Inc.: Excerpt from "Ripple" words by Robert Hunter. Copyright © 1971 by Ice Nine Publishing Company, Inc. Reprinted by permission.
Williamson Music Company: Excerpt from "You'll Never Walk Alone" by Richard Rodgers and Oscar Hammerstein II. Copyright 1945 by Williamson Music Co. Copyright renewed. Used by permission. All rights reserved.

Library of Congress Cataloging-in-Publication Data
Boyd, Blanche M., [date]
The revolution of little girls / Blanche McCrary Boyd.
p. cm.
ISBN 0-679-40090-7
I. Title.
PS3552.O8775R48   1991
813'.54—dc20   90-53545   CIP

Manufactured in the United States of America
First Edition

for Donna, and
for my brother Charlie

If I knew the way,
I would take you home.

—THE GRATEFUL DEAD, *"Ripple"*

Acknowledgments

I am grateful to more people than I can name, but some of them are: M. Mark, William Meredith, Susan Richards Shreve, Donna Tobias, Kim Phillips, Janet Gezari, Lisa Alther, Phyllis Rose, Anne Sibbald, Gary Fisketjon, and all the friends of Bill Wilson.

For the last eight years, my colleagues in the English Department at Connecticut College have provided me with a working environment that has been intellectually and creatively nourishing.

A grant from the National Endowment for the Arts furnished financial support at a crucial time.

I offer special thanks to my brother, Charles F. McCrary, who wrote the short story "John's Song," included as part of this novel.

The Revolution of Little Girls

Chapter 1

After the Tarzan serial at the movies every Saturday afternoon, my friend Hutch and I would climb the mimosa tree in his backyard and take off our shirts and eat bananas. Neither of us wanted to play Jane. I would sometimes consent if we could get my cousin Scooter to play Cheetah.

A rope "vine" was tied to a branch so we could swing to the ground. I was only eight years old—Hutch was nine, Scooter five—but I knew to put my shirt back on whenever we descended from the pink blossoms of the mimosa tree. The real world was suspicious of girls who did not want to play Jane.

I was not interested in Jane, but I was not willing to take the risks that Hutch did, either. Hutch ran away from school all through the first and second grades, and although his father whipped him—serious whippings that left welts on his legs—he kept doing it. I was a good girl in school, once I stopped crying. (For the first three months of first grade, I cried every day.) But Hutch injected grasshoppers with a

3

hypodermic needle he'd gotten from his aunt who was a nurse, and he set the grass in his yard on fire with a magnifying glass, and he had his own tonsils in a glass jar in his room—another present from his aunt. Hutch was bad, and I did whatever he told me to, if I thought I could get away with it. When I couldn't, my parents preferred lectures to beatings.

Mimosa blossoms smelled like candy, and if you ate a banana while you were surrounded by them, the sweetness got dizzying. One June afternoon, Hutch finished his banana and dropped the peel to Scooter, who was dragging his arms along the ground and saying *oooo-ga, ooo-ga,* his monkey sound. "Jane, cook dinner." Hutch thrust my shirt at me and patted the Bowie knife strapped at his waist. "I have to get that alligator."

I shoved at his arm and the shirt fell to the ground.

"Cheetah," Hutch ordered, "bring me that leopard skin."

Scooter put the shirt over his head and continued dragging his arms around, making his monkey sounds.

"I don't get any respect around here," Hutch said.

I held out my arm, indicating the blond hair on my forearm. Hutch held his forearm out beside mine. His arm was sturdier, the sun-bleached hair thicker. Our skin was warm and dry where it touched. "Brothers," I said, pointing at the still-raw scratches we had made on our arms and held against each other like thin mouths.

"Somebody has to be Jane," he said. Prestige was involved—Jane was not a hero—as well as adventure: Tarzan had more fun. Besides, boys didn't play at being girls, except

4

for Brad Thompson, who lived down the street. I had traded him my bride doll for his six-shooter, a transaction that improved my reputation and ruined his.

Hutch's nipples were tiny buttons, perfectly formed. Mine were pale and shriveled, like white raisins. Sitting on the branch of the mimosa tree, I reached out and touched one of his. Just as delicately, he felt one of mine. I said, "Go get that alligator."

Later that summer, when I was sent to camp, I wrote Hutch gawky love letters—*Dear Hutch, I will love you forever*—but had the good sense not to mail them. I knew I was just homesick. At camp you had to wear shoes, and what was the point of summer if you had to wear shoes? So one night a counselor found me wandering through the woods scream-ing for my mother, and the next day I was sent home.

The next year my parents bought a summer house, a little cabin on a big lake fifty miles from our home in Charleston, and Hutch's parents bought one too. Our families ate most of their meals together, along with Scooter and his parents and his brother and sister. Scooter's father was my mother's brother, and their family lived next door. Hutch lived a few doors away, but we all used the same boats, two small Bos-ton Whalers. We got Whalers, my father said, because they couldn't be turned over, and if they somehow were, they wouldn't sink.

When Hutch and I weren't fishing—we'd sometimes get up at dawn to catch bream off the dock, or sit out there after dark, hoping for large-mouth bass—we liked to scratch each other's backs. We were always sitting beside each other in

our bathing suits, taking turns scratching. The adults seemed
to find this charming. I loved the stupor Hutch's hand on my
back induced, the languor I could feel in him as I dragged my
nails across his shoulders.

When I was twelve I started menstruating, and there were
days I was not allowed to go into the water. Hutch, perhaps
warned by his mother, treated my nonswimming days re-
spectfully, as a mystery. My breasts were no longer pale
raisins but swelled under my bathing suit, and I hated how
my face felt if Hutch glanced at them.

This was the first year we could take the boat out by
ourselves. We had to stay close to shore, because in bad
weather the lake could be nearly as wild as the ocean. Hutch
and I would take the boat down past the pavilion, where we
liked to play pinball on Saturday nights, to a place we called
Bart's Cove.

The adults didn't know about Bart's Cove, and they
wouldn't have let us go there if they had. The lake was
man-made, a flooded valley, left unfinished at the outbreak
of World War II. Parts of it were studded with treacherous
stumps; in a few places the woods had not been leveled at
all. In Bart's Cove dead trees still stood in the water, and lazy
snakes hung in the trees.

Hutch and I were drawn by the secrecy and danger in
Bart's Cove, the snakes slipping off the trees with quiet
plops, disappearing under the skin of the water, and we were
drawn by the fish traps that someone had set and marked
with small red buoys. Most traps were out in the open areas
of the lake, and robbing them was conspicuously illegal. In

the privacy of Bart's Cove the thrill of pulling up the trap ropes like giant fishing lines became irresistible. If we found a few bream or crappies or a large catfish, what could be the harm in taking them?

I had my period and we were both sunburned. "But why can't you tell me?" Hutch asked again.

"I just can't, that's all."

Surrounded by trees, the cove felt airless in the July afternoon. We were both slick with sweat, and twice Hutch had flung himself out of the boat to cool off. He was quick getting back in because the snakes made even the bravest person cautious.

"I don't care if you can't swim, but why can't you tell me?"

This was the despair of physiology. My mother's explanations of menstruation were fine, but in my heart I knew I was wounded. I was bleeding from my sex, and it had to be a wound. Hutch was mounded and shaped at the crotch, his belly was hard and flat, but I was cut and swollen, and it was going to be this way every month until I was too old to care. Wearing shoes and going to school were nothing compared to what had happened inside me. "We're not catching anything," I said, which was how we always ended up robbing the traps.

Our anger and separation were in the air as we pulled up the muddy rope and wedged the first trap against the boat. "Get it in! Get it in!" Hutch shouted, while I lifted the wire cage over the side. The brown water had hidden the contents of the cage, and I dumped it onto the bottom of the boat and

.opened the door in one motion. A dead bass fell out, a few bream, and a large snake.

The snake seemed as dazed as we were. We scrambled to stand side by side on the boards of the rear seat while it slithered to the bow of the boat and curled up. Lazily it opened its whitish mouth at us. "Jesus," Hutch said, "it's a cottonmouth."

"Jesus, what are we going to do?"

"Jesus," Hutch said again. Then—perhaps remembering his training as Tarzan—he said, "Jesus isn't here," and picked up the oar to do battle with the snake.

I grabbed his arm in midair. "It's my period! I'm having my period!"

"We've got a snake in the boat!" he shouted, but I'd begun to cry. "That blood stuff?" he said uncertainly, lowering the paddle. "That's horrible." He put his arm around me.

We stood on the boat seat a long time, because Tarzan had lost the courage of his original impulse, and the snake seemed happy and even fell asleep. Anyway, neither of us could think of anything to say or do.

When the sun was setting and we knew our parents would be worried, Hutch took the paddle, gingerly lifted the snake, and dropped him into the dark water. I would have stood on that boat seat all night.

The girl who lived next door at the lake was seventeen, and her father was a captain in the Navy. Nancy had found a stack of sexy novels in his study, so, while her parents were at work each day, Hutch and I joined her for lengthy reading sessions. Our parents wondered why we had lost interest in water skiing and fishing.

Nancy was a homely girl, but she had long, elegant legs and fascinating breasts. She smoked cigarettes, and sometimes she let Hutch and me smoke too. She taught us to kiss by demonstrating on our arms. "Keep your tongue between your lips but don't be pushy," she advised, moving her wet mouth mechanically against my wrist.

These novels weren't actually pornographic. The sex scenes shied away from any mention of genitals, coming no closer than the line *He was inside her.* Nancy and Hutch and I would read quietly to ourselves, then pass the books around, sharing the good parts. After a few hours we would all go into separate bedrooms to "take naps." I didn't know what to do with the excitement and pleasure I felt. Sometimes I would touch myself, but my notions were vague and dreamlike, and usually I slept.

One afternoon when Nancy was swimming, Hutch and I lay on her sofa in our bathing suits and scratched each other's backs. I kept thinking of a picture on one of the book jackets: a woman in a blue peignoir. Hutch seemed more tentative than usual, and I was aware of the length of his bare leg against mine.

He lay on his stomach, his arms folded under his head, while I rubbed his brown back. "I hope I never get zits," I said. "I hope I never get crippled. I hope I never have to have a nose job."

"Have you ever done it?" he asked.

9

My hand stopped moving. "Done what?" Self-con-
sciously I began to scratch again. "Why, have you?"

"Of course. Almost all the boys in eighth grade have."

The inside of my mouth felt like paper. "Who with?"

I could feel him trembling. "It wouldn't be right to tell."

"I'm going swimming with Nancy," I said, sitting up.

School started, and we moved back into town from the lake.
Fall was a tingle in the skin, a coolness in the lungs, a football
tossed around the front yard. I was the only girl anyone
knew who could throw a spiral—in fact, the only girl allowed to play. Hutch would announce, "She plays, want to
make anything of it?" and of course no one did.

We built a cabin in Hutch's backyard. It was small and
ramshackle, tacked together out of odd boards. A plate-size
window was cut in one side, and cloth curtains hung over the
window and the door, which you had to crawl through. The
cabin was comfortable for two or three people to sit in,
though not tall enough for us to stand.

One afternoon we took blankets out to the cabin, and a
deck of cards and match sticks. We collected Scooter for
safety, for a kind of chaperon, and then we played strip
poker.

We weren't quite sure how to play strip poker, although
we understood five-card draw. Actually, Scooter didn't.
Scooter, whose real name was Paul, was a weird boy with
large front teeth and a crew cut. He had been diagnosed as
retarded in the first grade because he pretended he couldn't

read without empty eye-glass frames on his face. He was doing better in school now, but he still wrote backwards unless he concentrated. The numbers on the cards mixed him up. In our poker game, Hutch and I protected him. It wasn't Scooter we were interested in seeing without his clothes.

After I'd lost my shoes and socks and sweater, I slipped my bra off without taking off my shirt.

Dusk was falling, and Hutch lit a candle, and the light in the cabin changed. I was sitting with my bra stuffed under my leg so no one could look at it too closely. "You better not tell," I whispered to Scooter. I didn't know what I could take off next, but I was sweaty and thrilled with the problem.

My cards got comically good, and Hutch began to lose. He lost his shoes and his shirt and his silver I.D. bracelet and his father's dog tag from World War II. Only his pants were left.

I got dealt four queens. No need to draw. I laid down my hand.

Hutch hesitated and blew out the candle. "Cover your eyes," he said to me. He whispered to Scooter, "You better not tell." Then he raised himself up on his knees and dropped his pants.

I peeked through my fingers expecting to see his underpants, but he had lowered them too, and I glimpsed his thick, reddish penis. Dark hairs were scrambled all around it. I snapped the windows of my fingers closed, instantly full of regret.

Hutch pulled his pants back up. "You can look now," he said, as if I hadn't already done so. We were all cold and

11

miserable with embarrassment. It was dark out, and the game was over.

When I tried to sleep that night, the darkness of my room was full of slick black snakes opening their whitish mouths, and the band of light at the base of my door, coming from where my mother and father sat in the den watching television, looked gold and warm and safe. When I closed my eyes I began to cry because of the snakes, and soon the crying got louder, and my mother came to my room to see what was wrong.

My mother was nice to me, touching my hair as I mumbled about cottonmouths, but the crying was like another person inside me who kept choking and coughing. I shouted, "We don't catch all those fish! We rob the fish traps!" My mother stroked me, forgiving me, but I still couldn't bear it, so I shouted, "Nancy gives us dirty novels to read!" My mother's hand hesitated as she assessed this information. She said she didn't think books like that were a good idea, and she had some other books for me that she should have given me sooner. I shouted, "We played strip poker in the cabin and Hutch took off his pants!"

My mother's composure snapped like wire. She was out of my room, then out the back door before I could stop her.

The lights were on at Hutch's house, and I could hear Hutch's mother screaming, "He's just a little boy! For God's sake, Jack, he's a little boy! He won't do it again! Hutch, tell him you won't do it again!"

Even my father stuck his head in my room briefly, to see what was wrong. "Nothing," I said. "Nothing is wrong."

My mother came back and sat on the bed with me. I was not crying now. I thought I hated my mother. We were listening to Hutch's mother sobbing—the whole neighborhood was.

In the morning I heard the sounds of our cabin being dismantled: hammering, and the screech of boards being pried apart. Staring out our bathroom window, I watched Hutch in his backyard.

I went into my backyard and looked at him across the fence. He put down his hammer and looked back at me. His face was swollen, and one eye was turning black. "I'm sorry," I said.

He said nothing, turning back to his work.

Hutch and I didn't talk about this incident for many years. At first we didn't speak at all. Then, a few months after our poker game, my family moved to the country, away from the house where he and I had been next-door neighbors. Soon after we moved, my father was killed in an accident. My life diverged from Hutch's and from nearly everything else I was familiar with.

Hutch and I went to different high schools. We still spent our summers at the lake, but we now looked at each other across a great sexual gulf. Hutch was surrounded by raucous, angry boys, and I was immersed in grief and isolation. There were, I had decided, three categories in the world: men, women, and me.

Hutch hung around with his friends down at the pavilion,

smoking cigarettes and playing pinball, his father's dog tag still dangling from his neck. I went to summer school, driving the fifty miles back into Charleston with my head hanging out the car window to keep me awake.

Graduating from high school a year early, I went to college at Duke, where I surprised everyone, including myself, by getting married. I met my husband the summer after my freshman year, at Harvard Summer School. Nicky had thick glasses and pale skin and I thought he was a genius.

In the summer of 1966, we stayed at the beach house for a week with my family. One afternoon Nicky went out fishing with Scooter. I was sitting under the big oak tree by the boat ramp, gazing out at the humid, silvery afternoon. Using binoculars, I could see our new Whaler—a sixteen-footer—outlined against the purple horizon. I was wearing my bathing suit but hadn't been in the water.

Hutch slipped into the beach chair beside me. I glanced at him and looked farther into his eyes than I meant to. He gave me a light smile, so I stared down at his muscled chest. It was tanned, and punctuated by familiar nipples. That wasn't the right place to look either.

"You shouldn't have told," he said.

"I know." I twisted an eyepiece on the binoculars. "I guess I went kind of crazy."

"My dad beat the hell out of me."

"I know." I squinted down at the binoculars. "I'm so sorry, Hutch."

"I know."

I kept squinting down at the binoculars, and he reached

over and picked up my hand. "Girls always get something
in their eye," he said.

Soon we went into the water, which was as lukewarm as
a bath you've drawn and forgotten to get into. Hutch said,
about my husband, "He's okay, really," and I said, "He's
very smart." Hutch's eyes were directly blue, and the muscles in his neck moved when he laughed. He looked like a
hero.

Hutch told me how much he hated the military college his
father had sent him to. He'd been thrown out twice for
insubordination, and his draft notice had arrived. In the fall,
he'd be in Vietnam.

The next time I talked with Hutch, seven more years had
passed, and I was tripping on mescaline at my mother's
Christmas party. I was divorced and had recently proclaimed
myself a lesbian revolutionary in a twenty-four-page letter
to my mother, who was not happy with this news. For the
first time I felt lucky that my father had died.

I knew a little bit about what had happened to Hutch. He
had returned from Vietnam with a Purple Heart and a
Bronze Star, had finished at his military college, and had
married a woman who dropped out of medical school for
him. Now he worked in a bank.

My mother's Christmas party involved a compromise. I
was currently refusing to shave my legs or armpits, so I wore
a long-sleeved black silk shirt and black silk pants. Having
consented to earrings, I actually looked quite good.

Two hundred people had been invited to this annual event, which once had been held in a circus tent with three blinking trees on top. This year it was in the Masonic Temple. My mother wanted me to stand next to her in the receiving line, so I took the mescaline.

Hutch came in wearing a cheap blue suit, his hand on his pregnant wife's back. Hutch's hair was thinning, and he seemed angry. He introduced me to Merle, a pretty and surprisingly serious-looking woman. I watched him seat her at one of the long tables, then stride back towards me.

"Get your coat," he commanded.

Obediently I headed for the coatroom, calling over my shoulder to my mother, "I'm going outside to talk to Hutch."

She dropped a very short man's hand and followed me into the vestibule. "Honey, you can't go outside with him. He's here with his wife."

My mother's face had grown harsher in the last year. She had recently buried her third husband, but on some level I think she was still waiting for my father to get home from work.

"Mom, don't be so bourgeois." The mescaline made the planes in her face move, the dots in her eyes swim around. I tried not to focus as I put on my coat.

"Honey, I'm talking about common decency. Think of how Merle feels. . . ." But I had stopped listening and was quickly through the swinging glass doors, out to where Hutch stood waiting.

The wind was colder than I'd thought, and the drug made the night seem bitter. Hutch's face was rigid, and his blue eyes blinked rapidly. "What is all this communist crap? My mother says you've turned radical. I've been fighting the goddamn communists and you're out getting arrested. You are screwing up your life! You're screwing up!"

I realized the whole truth was not circulating yet, and I didn't know whether to be angry with my mother or glad for her discretion. Tears formed in my eyes. "I'm screwing up!" I shouted. "You're a banker, and you think I'm screwing up?"

He grabbed me by the shoulders. "What's wrong with being a banker?"

"Lots is wrong with it! Lots."

Hutch kissed me, standing right there on the sidewalk. His mouth felt toothy and hard, but I felt the great relief in both of us. After all, we'd been waiting to do this all our lives.

When I stopped crying, we sat on a park bench. Hutch slipped his arm around me, the way he had when we were standing on the boat seat. "We've got to go back to the party," he said. "Let's have lunch tomorrow. Nobody has to know."

We met the next day at the Piggy Park, for the barbecue buffet. When we went through the line, Hutch piled up his plate. "That's all you're going to eat?" he said. I noticed how he'd thickened: His face was fuller, and his belly swelled slightly above his belt.

At first we were distant and noncommittal. I drank a beer to take the edge off the post-mescaline letdown while we tried to think of things to say. Then the left's newest lesbian inquired, "Are you happy with Merle?"

Hutch was eating an ear of corn that dripped butter. "I thought she'd make a good wife," he finally said.

"But are you happy, Hutch?"

"Are you?"

When I didn't answer, he chewed, looking at me. "I'll show you our house."

Hutch's house was a small suburban box, as cluttered as the houses we'd lived in as children. Merle's doll collection dotted one wall, Hutch's guns adorned another.

Hutch sat in a La-Z-Boy chair and stared down at the knees of his polyester pants, the tassels of his loafers. "When I got back from Vietnam, I just wanted to be normal. So I looked around for who would make me the best wife. And I picked Merle. Merle's great."

I sat at the Formica table in the breakfast nook studying the red-flecked pattern. "I don't have any birth control with me."

He didn't look at me. "Merle's great, Ellen."

"Why'd you tell me you'd slept with girls?"

"To impress you."

"You scared me."

He shrugged in a way I remembered.

"I've got to go, Hutch. I can't handle this."

He stood up, looking relieved. "Don't be a communist," he said. "It's silly."

Hutch and I had our last serious conversation a number of years later. I had exchanged being a revolutionary for being

a television writer in Hollywood. Hutch had become an of-
ficer in his bank. He and Merle had three children, all girls.

I was home visiting my mother at the beach house, and the
families all had a fish fry together. Scooter had just bought
the Chrysler dealership in North Charleston, and he kept
shaking hands with everyone, even his own relatives.
"Someday he'll run General Motors," my mother said. She
had recently dyed her hair a butter yellow.

Hutch had run to fat, and most of his hair was gone. Merle
was going to Weight Watchers and looked smart, though
nervous about me, as always. I had recently graduated from
my first treatment center for drug addiction and alcoholism,
but my family didn't know about that. Because I was swimming half a mile daily instead of drinking, I looked better
than I had in a long time.

Age was making my mother ornery. "You're worse than
those actresses," she said, watching me do calisthenics. My
mother always thinks, if I'm unhappy, that it's over a lover.
"You act like you're in heat."

"I'm just doing exercises, Momma. Anyway, it doesn't feel
much like heat."

Late at night I saw Hutch out on our dock, fishing. Everyone seemed to have gone to bed, so I joined him.

On the horizon, beyond an island where we'd once pic-
nicked, glowed the Hydron Power Plant, dark orange, like a
sinister sunset. Strobe lights flashed among the smooth
buildings, which looked both prehistoric and space age,
oddly beautiful.

Hutch was sitting on the ladder, casting. There was no

breeze. The water was greenish within the perimeter of the dock lights, black beyond.

I fastened a slender rubber worm to my line, stood at the rail, cast, then began to drag my bait slowly across the bottom. "Anything biting?"

Hutch glanced at me. "Saw a big bass, but he wasn't interested."

After a few minutes, I said, "The power plant looks like the stones at the end of the world."

"You take too many drugs," Hutch said. He was finishing a beer.

"I'm trying not to take them anymore, but maybe what they do to you is permanent."

"If you could find the end of the world," he said.

I sat beside him on the ladder. He was wearing cutoffs and a knit shirt that stretched across his stomach.

We were quiet for a while, fishing. Then Hutch said, "Can I tell you something I never told anybody?"

"If you want to."

"In Vietnam, I did something really bad."

There was a lot I could have asked, but I didn't. "Everybody's done something really bad, Hutch."

He shook his head, and I watched the muscles in his jaw working.

"I'm sorry" was all I said.

"I am too. That's what I have. That I'm sorry." He picked up my hand and held it, and our lines hung slack in the water. We stared at the power plant's dark orange glow, and then, after a while, we began to fish. We might have gone to bed together, but there was no place for us. Hutch and Merle were staying at his family's house, and I was staying at mine.

At dawn Merle came walking across the lawn. She was wearing a blue peignoir. "Hutch, what are you doing down here?"

"Coming home." He reeled in his line, fastened the rubber worm to the rod, then got up and walked toward her. He didn't look back.

There's not much else to tell about Hutch except that, last August, when I went home to take care of my mother during her facelift, I saw him briefly at the beach. My mother and I have achieved a delicate peace, mostly because I've been sober and drug-free for a number of years now. She was recovering nicely at her condominium in town, so I'd driven up to the lake house to pick up some things for her, take a sunbath, maybe visit with Scooter.

Hutch and Merle and their youngest daughter, Anne, were down by the dock. Anne was on crutches. Hutch said she'd tried to dive from the roof of their utility room into their pool, and her left foot didn't quite make it. "She's wild," Hutch said.

"She's the one who sucked her toes when she was a baby," said Merle, who no longer seemed threatened by me.

"Anne's so much like you," Hutch said.

"I wasn't the wild one."

I studied this Anne, whose blond hair and scarred chin,

from a fall on the boat ramp when she was little, seemed part of some message I couldn't quite decipher.

Later, when Anne and I were lying on the dock together, sunbathing, I said, "Your father and I used to play Tarzan and Jane together in a tree in his yard."

She blinked at me suspiciously. Grownups, to her, were like cardboard cutouts, part of the backdrop of her life. "My cast itches," she said.

"Your father once had a cast on his arm. . . ."

"It just itches," she said.

Before sunset I went fishing with Scooter, who had recently bought a twenty-two foot Whaler with a two hundred horsepower motor. It had begun to seem terribly important to me to catch a fish. If I could catch a fish, maybe I wouldn't feel this hot, surprising loss.

Rockfish travel in schools. They chase shad, and if you can get to the school while they're still breaking the surface and can manage to throw out a line without hooking yourself or falling out of the boat, you'll probably catch one. The excitement is in finding the schools and getting into them in time.

Scooter and I were sitting in the gray center of the lake for less than half an hour before we spotted a large churning patch of white water about a mile away from us. We raced furiously into the middle of it, but Scooter promptly fouled the line of his new rod and began to swear. I hooked and landed a ten-pound bass.

The fish, once in the boat, seemed disappointing. The silver light reflecting off it was real enough, but the way this light entered me was an illusion, a wish. Hutch and I were past forty, and to his daughter I was just a lady visiting down the beach.

I put the fish into the Styrofoam cooler and stared down at it, glittering.

"I have bad *luck*," Scooter said. His new motor wouldn't start, and the school of fish had come back up just out of reach. He was crouched by the gas tanks, trying to make the coupling to the motor hold. "You can ask anybody. With mechanical things I have bad *luck*."

Scooter, who is called Paul now, is the most powerful automobile dealer in the South. He is married to a pediatrician, and they have two sons. But Paul's car phone doesn't work, and the heating system in his house developed so many leaks the walls had to be torn out to repair it.

"You have bad luck." I bit my thumbnail so hard it started to bleed. I was in this boat with Paul, and Hutch was on the dock a few miles away. His hair was nearly gone, his paunch was hanging over his bathing suit, and his blue eyes were embedded in the puffiness of his face like old stones, like jewels in some crumbling god that Tarzan might have found in his jungle, with the poor dumb natives kneeling before it.

I will love you forever, I wrote to Hutch, and I have told this lie too many times to too many people. But standing in the boat with Paul, I understood that when Hutch reached through the branches of the mimosa tree and touched my breast, the blue arc of feeling that leapt between us stayed inside me. It was like the fish in this cooler, something pulled from deep water.

I knelt down beside the fish, and it gazed up at me, panting slightly. "Thank you so much," I whispered.

"It's not your fault," Paul mumbled, "it's the damn mechanic's."

The gas coupling was fixed, but the skin of the water was smooth, without any sign of schools.

We watched the sun disappear behind a cloud bank. The power plant's strobe light began to flash against the twilight. I climbed into the driver's seat beside Paul. On the depth finder we could see red blips, echoes.

Paul said, "We'd better get back, Ellen. Nothing else is going to happen out here."

We rode slowly back across the lake, and I sat on the cooler that held my fish.

Chapter 2

When I was in the eleventh grade, my English teacher, Mr. Endicott, dropped his college ring down Reggie Lucas's shirt, then reached inside to retrieve it. Mr. Endicott had been to military college and perhaps thought such behavior could be passed off as horseplay.

He'd been reading *Our Town* to us out loud. Most students at Plaxton High majored in Home Economics or Agriculture, and Mr. Endicott had been teaching at Plaxton High for fifteen years. At some point in his career he had probably discussed literature and assigned papers, but by the time I was in his class, we diagrammed sentences on the blackboard or else he read to us. There was no point in giving us assignments, because we wouldn't do them.

In the first act of *Our Town*, a typical day in Grover's Corners, New Hampshire, is described. I was as bored by Mr. Endicott's droning as everyone else when Reggie Lucas raised his hand. "Bill," he said winningly, "are you sure you went to VMI? Do they even *have* English majors at VMI?"

Reggie smiled, baring large white teeth. We were not allowed to call Mr. Endicott by his first name.

Reggie had a blond, waxed flattop and the most attractive collarbones I had ever seen. We'd ridden together in the back seat of a car the week before, all the way home from a basketball tournament. My friend Marla had arranged this. Reggie wasn't very interested in me sexually but found Marla's invitation worth exploring. In the car he kissed me several times, and I was so thrilled to have my fantasy fulfilled that I couldn't actually feel anything. "I just don't want to do this," Reggie said, nibbling wetly on my neck. "I've got to play again tomorrow night." I kissed him back woodenly, worried about what to do with my tongue. "Jesus," he groaned after a while, leaning back and pointing to the crotch of his warmup pants. "You've done it to me now. This is your fault."

"What?" I said, refusing to look down.

"I *knew* this would happen," he said. *"Look* at it."

I stared hard at the couple in the front seat, who were pretending to be deaf. "Reggie," I said, suddenly inspired, "what do you think of Mr. Endicott?"

"He's a queer," Reggie snarled at the fogged window beside him. "Everybody knows that."

"But what do you think of him?"

"I think he's a queer."

I decided to try a different approach. "If you could have anything in the world you wanted, what would it be?"

He looked darkly hopeful. "I'll show you," he said, grabbing my wrist.

I snatched my hand away. "Really, Reggie. What would you want?"

"A Corvette," he said and folded his arms across his chest. He shut his eyes and pretended to sleep.

Outside the other back window, which was unfogged by Reggie's distress, I watched the dark South Carolina landscape slide by, catching glimpses of Spanish moss in live oak trees, dense stands of pine, the shacks where black people lived. White people's houses were few. The rural Lowcountry was mostly black, and the schools had not yet been integrated. Our district was over thirty miles long. The trips to ball games were tedious. I felt disappointed and embarrassed about Reggie, so I composed a new note for Mr. Endicott:

> *When you're driving your car*
> *and relief seems so far*
> *remember that suffering is always random*
> *but you are protected by your friend*
> *the Phantom.*

I had begun these notes a few weeks before. The first one I left on the dashboard of his car. After that I scribbled them on his blackboard, before class. He seemed very happy about them. "I have an admirer," he'd say.

Mr. Endicott was a tall, masculine man, but his buttocks were a bit thick, probably from sitting down for fifteen years, and he had a generous mouth. "I know what he does with those rubber lips," I once heard Reggie's friend Cliff say.

In English class Reggie flirted contemptuously with Mr. Endicott, both to entertain the rest of us and to stall the readings. Mr. Endicott was intrigued by Reggie's insolence, and he usually stopped whatever he was doing to smile and chat.

"VMI was tougher than the army, Reggie," he said. "I promise you it was tougher than playing basketball."

"Why weren't *you* in the army?" Cliff asked. He was a burly boy with small, blinky eyes.

Mr. Endicott smiled. "Somebody had to bring y'all some culture."

Perhaps this is why I liked Mr. Endicott: he could be sarcastic and pleasant at the same time.

"Cliff," Mr. Endicott said, "you aren't by any chance the Phantom, are you?"

"Nah," Cliff said, "it's Reggie."

I was hurt by this exchange, because neither Cliff nor Reggie was smart enough to rhyme anything, even partially.

"Let me see your ring," Reggie said.

Mr. Endicott hesitated, then rose from his desk and walked toward him. Maybe he just wanted to stand next to him. I could understand that. He handed Reggie his ring.

Reggie examined it and threw it to Cliff, whose chair was next to mine.

Mr. Endicott didn't know what to do, so he just stood there awkwardly. After a few seconds, Cliff threw the ring back, and Mr. Endicott's hand snatched it out of the air right in front of Reggie's.

Reggie grabbed Mr. Endicott's wrist and they struggled.

"Here, if you want it so much," Mr. Endicott said, and he dropped the ring down the back of Reggie's shirt.

We were very quiet except for the sound of our breathing. It was English class and something wrong had happened. No one knew what to do.

"I'll get it," Mr. Endicott said, resuming his grown-up teacher's tone. He reached his hand matter-of-factly inside Reggie's shirt.

Reggie leaped from his seat, and I could see him trembling. He pulled out his shirttail and the ring hit the linoleum floor with a brief, muffled sound. It rolled toward me and stopped right by my penny loafer. I picked it up. It was a heavy gold school ring with a blue stone.

Mr. Endicott looked grateful as I handed it to him. He went back to his desk and took up reading *Our Town* again.

It's hard to explain what happened next. The class was so tense and unnerved that we began to listen desperately to the play. Dr. Gibbs was chastising his son George for not doing his chores and leaving his mother to chop wood. *Our Town* was set in 1900, but I didn't think that could account for all the differences from Plaxton that I was noticing. My father had died in an automobile accident; Reggie's father was a butcher at Mack's Meats; Cliff's father was our town doctor and, as everyone knew, he beat his son—that's where the scars on Cliff's back came from.

When Dr. Gibbs got disgruntled because Mrs. Gibbs was staying too long at choir practice, I began to giggle. The women on the way home from choir practice had stopped on the corner to gossip about the town drunk: "Really," one of them said, "it's the worst scandal that ever was in this town!"

I was trying to stop giggling when Mrs. Gibbs arrived home and Dr. Gibbs complained, "You're late enough," and Mrs. Gibbs replied, "Now, Frank, don't be grouchy. Come out and smell my heliotrope in the moonlight."

I started to laugh out loud. I didn't know what heliotrope was, and this remark struck me as hilariously off-color.

Mr. Endicott stopped reading. I put my head down on the desk but I knew he was looking at me. "Try to get hold of yourself, Ellen." The pleasant sarcasm was back in his voice.

But this laughter was like nothing that had ever happened to me. My face felt hot, and my new contact lenses were floating off my eyes. I gripped the edges of my desk as Mr. Endicott continued to read.

A few minutes later Mr. Webb, Dr. Gibbs's neighbor, went up to his daughter's room to see why she wasn't in bed. "I just can't sleep yet, Papa," she said. "The moonlight's so *won-*derful. And the smell of Mrs. Gibbs's heliotrope. Can you smell it?"

A howling noise escaped me. I began to pound helplessly on my desk.

"My dear," Mr. Endicott said, "heliotrope is a flower."

I stood up, squinting to hold my lenses in place. I could hardly breathe, much less speak. The laughter was brutalizing me with its terrible release, and I was no longer sure if I was laughing or crying.

Now Mr. Endicott sounded concerned. "Do you want to go home, my dear?"

I pulled my books against my chest, nodding.

"Go by the office."

I struggled down the hallway, still laughing, my face soaked with tears. In the principal's office I couldn't speak so I wrote a note to the secretary and pushed it across her desk: GOING HOME. CAN'T STOP LAUGHING.

Seven years passed.

Reggie married Marla's other friend, Janine. He inherited Mack's Meats, and he and Janine had two children. Soon after birth the girl died of spinal meningitis; the boy was slow and timid.

Right out of high school Cliff surprised everyone by marrying Marla. He surprised everyone again by becoming a successful antique dealer in Charleston, thirty miles away from Plaxton. Cliff soon learned to talk comfortably and grammatically about Edwardian, Victorian, or antebellum, but on Sundays he remained content to watch ball games on TV with Reggie, while Marla and Janine made chili or fried chicken and pies with Cool Whip on top.

Mr. Endicott developed a hearing problem and had to give up teaching. He became a furniture restorer, a job he could do in his own garage. Sometimes he did freelance work for his former student, Cliff.

I moved to California and got enmeshed in a number of pursuits I considered radical and beautiful.

"It makes me want to throw up," my mother said, in reference to my newly declared homosexuality.

We were driving in her new Mercedes to the country club

to have dinner and play bingo. My mother did not really like the new Mercedes, so she was letting me drive it. She'd bought it because she could afford it, but a Datsun, she'd informed me as she handed me the keys, was definitely a superior car.

"You don't like this car because you've gained too much weight to be comfortable under the steering wheel," I said as we pulled out of the driveway of her condominium, past the guard house.

"The steering wheel is too large and it is incorrectly placed."

"I think the steering wheel's just fine."

My mother was wearing a red jersey dress and lots of gold jewelry. She admitted that she would limp tomorrow from her high heels. I was wearing a black dress and high heels, to prove to her that I still liked being a woman. I would probably limp tomorrow too.

We pulled into the country club lot and parked under the moss-draped arms of a huge live oak tree. When I came around the car to open her door and help her out, I kissed her on the cheek. "Does that make you want to throw up?"

My mother was shorter and heavier than me. The woman I changed my life over was taller and thinner, and embracing her was nothing like kissing my mother on the cheek.

She hugged me miserably. "Honey, I'm afraid people will try to hurt you about this."

"Me too, Momma. I'm afraid too."

"Couldn't you change your mind?"

"I don't think so." Over her shoulder, beyond the smooth green fairway, I watched the Ashley River slide turbidly by.

Cliff and Reggie were watching a different river through the plate-glass window in Reggie's den. "I always wanted to live on this river," Reggie said. He would say this every Sunday, but today there was something vague in his voice, something about loss.

"You did it, Bo." That was what Cliff always said too. But yesterday Cliff closed a deal on an eighteenth-century house in the historic area of Charleston. His voice was as wistful as Reggie's.

Reggie did not want Cliff to move away from Plaxton. He said that it was one thing to work in Charleston, but moving there was another. "It's too far from my store out here, Bo," Cliff said. "Ain't nobody in Plaxton gonna buy anty-cues."

Reggie closed the curtains. He was thinking about butchers' wounds. Butchers always sliced toward their abdomens, and sometimes they got cut. His father had cut himself once in twenty years, perforating his intestine, but it was lung cancer that killed him. "My daddy always wanted to live on this river."

My mother was winning at bingo. She was playing so many cards she had to put some on an extra chair beside the table. She mumbled for the caller, an adenoidal, bored young woman, to slow down. "Honey, why don't you tell her to slow down." My mother was too polite, herself, to complain to anyone directly.

"I'm too well brought up to do any such thing," I said, but when I walked up front to collect one of her $25 prizes, I conveyed her request. The girl gave me a bovine look and nodded. I wasn't quite sure what the nod meant. Southerners are as polite as cattle, except when they're not. When they're not, they might shoot you or chase you around the yard with a hatchet.

"Thank you, honey," my mother whispered, when I re-seated myself at the table.

Later, at home, she tied a pair of underpants around her head to protect her hairdo. "It just works better than anything else. I know it looks silly." In our pajamas we had a nightcap, bourbon for her, brandy for me, and kept the television running in the background. On the news was a picture of Bobby Seale tied to a chair with his mouth taped shut.

"My father's sister was . . ." my mother said. "Of course we didn't call it . . . we didn't call it anything."

"How did you know she was? You can call it gay."

"Well, she lived with another woman who was younger than she was, and she raised her child with her. Also, she was mannish."

"Do you think I'm mannish?"

"And Cousin Bryce, when he was going to marry that girl he brought home for Christmas? Then excused himself from dinner and went upstairs and shot himself with the shotgun? I think he was, too."

"Do you think I'm mannish?"

"I don't know what to think about you, Ellen. Gay seems like such an inappropriate word."

"Well, anyway, thank you for giving me the family history."

Reggie and Cliff were watching the same newscast: Bobby Seale's trial had been severed from that of the rest of the Chicago Eight, who were now the Chicago Seven. Popcorn was spilled across the coffee table. Marla and Janine were asleep on the sofa. Reggie and Cliff were drunk. "How'm I gonna get her into the car?" Cliff said.

"Look at that nigger," Reggie said, pointing at the television. "I tell you, I'm glad somebody burned the high school down. So much for having to go to school with them."

Cliff raised Marla's limp arm and dropped it. "I guess she's not driving."

"Remember those pig balls?" Reggie said. "Castrating pigs was about the only good thing we learned in Agriculture." He made a noise that was half-whispered but as high-pitched as a scream.

Janine stirred on the sofa without waking.

"If I close one eye I see fine," Cliff said. "Too bad I've got to drive with two."

"Remember how we left 'em on Endicott's doorstep? With a note from the Phantom? Old Endicott, old rubber lips. He probably thought it was a compliment. He probably thought that crazy girl did it. Ellen. The one who laughed."

Cliff was helping Marla to her feet. "Don't be so goddamn dumb, Reggie. Don't be such an asshole. Of course he knew we did it. Of course he knew that."

Three months after I returned to California, my lover left me and returned to her husband, a man who wore his shirts half buttoned, exposing a chestful of hair and gold chains. She grew her nails long again, and painted them red. "I just couldn't handle it," she said.

"It?" My lover had been a radical who said the word *lesbian* as easily as my mother said *segregation.* "What about being revolutionaries? What about custody of the cats?"

"My shrink says I was going through a phase. You can keep the cats."

We were standing close to each other, but I was looking at the poster of Emma Goldman on the wall behind her. "Don't you think you could've figured this out a bit sooner?"

For several months I stayed in bed listening to Linda Ronstadt records. Linda Ronstadt, I felt sure, understood suffering. I drank half gallons of wine, smoked marijuana, and inhaled hundreds of hits of laughing gas. Nitrous oxide is the propellant for whipped cream dispensers. Whippets, we called them. Dealers sold the cartridges with a small instrument that emptied them into balloons. I didn't laugh much, but my lungs developed enough to inhale an entire balloon in one breath.

· · ·

Mr. Endicott liked the mall. It was a safe place to walk, and his doctors had told him to exercise. He couldn't go to bars anymore because the music hurt his ears, and going to the Battery to cruise wasn't safe at his age. But in the bright artificial light of the mall he could walk and look. The smooth, careless bodies of the young seemed a kind of museum, and he felt harmless enough, looking. When he was tired, he would sit in the center of the mall by the fountain. The noise of the water was soothing.

My mother and I found him there, eating a cup of frozen yogurt.

Mr. Endicott was wearing a plaid wool shirt, and his gray hair was combed neatly. His eyes had the dreamy quality that the hard of hearing sometimes develop.

"Look," my mother said, "isn't that your old high school English teacher?"

My mother had recently had her facelift, and it was too soon for her to be out in public. She still looked bruised and puffy and garish. "Like Frankenstein," she'd said, cheerfully putting on her sweatsuit that morning. She had twelve identical sweatsuits, each in a different color. Today she was wearing powder pink, topped with dark glasses.

I was holding my mother's elbow. "Yes. It is." When she'd asked me to take care of her during her recovery, I was both troubled and touched. I was taking my duties seriously.

"Hello there, stranger!" my mother said gaily, seizing Mr. Endicott's hand. "Look who's come home!"

Mr. Endicott seemed alarmed because he didn't recognize either of us at first. I'd been out of high school twenty-five years. I wasn't sure he'd ever met my mother; at any rate, she looked as if she'd been beaten up in a barroom fight.

"Ellen?" Mr. Endicott's eyes were watery and vulnerable. "Is that you?"

"One and the same," I said.

He fumbled with his yogurt cup. "My stars. I thought you would never come back to South Carolina. I thought you were too big for us."

"She is! She is!" my mother said. "She's written a best-seller cookbook and even a screenplay! She's come home to help me with my facelift! Don't I look like Frankenstein?"

"Do you remember my mother?" I said.

Late the next afternoon I drove out toward Plaxton in my mother's Mercedes. The car was seventeen years old, seasoned and comfortable, and, according to my mother, the best car she'd ever had. The offending steering wheel had been replaced by a mahogany Nardi she'd ordered from the Beverly Hills Motoring Accessories catalog.

The road across the marshes had become a divided highway. At the Plaxton River, I noticed that the huge oak that used to hang into the water was gone. The banks had been cleared, and where the tree once was a small ranch house now stood. The house had a picture window, but the curtains were closed.

Past Plaxton, the road became the familiar two-lane blacktop crowded by fecund brush. In clearings were the same old shacks or small brick houses. A black snake slithered across the pavement. In the distance the road looked wet and shiny. "It's a mirage," my father had told me when I was a little girl. "The heat causes it." I had loved the word *mirage* and would say it over and over, gazing at the end of the road.

In Plaxton, the Chevrolet dealership still looked as if it only stocked two or three cars. The drugstore was boarded up, but a combination convenience store and gas station was new. Mack's Meats had expanded from a small cinderblock building to a larger cinderblock building.

I pulled in beside the phone booth near the gas pumps at the convenience store and sat there for a few minutes. It was cool in the air-conditioned car, but I was sweating. Finally I got out and called my home in Vermont.

Meg's voice, husky and mocking, answered on the tape machine: "This is Tammy Faye Bakker. Jim and I can't come to the phone right now, because we're praying over my hairdo."

"Meg," I said after the beep, "I hate these damn phone jokes. Anyway, picture this. I'm standing in a parking lot across from Mack's Meats in Plaxton, South Carolina, and a boy I was ferociously attracted to in high school is probably over there working. It's damn hot. I'm going to dinner tonight at my high school English teacher's house. I'll call back tonight. I miss you."

The asphalt was sticky under my tennis shoes.

There were no customers in the store. "Is Reggie around?"

I asked the girl behind the counter. Slight and bored, she looked familiar. One of the Glendennings, I decided. She directed me through a doorway to Reggie's cluttered office.

He was sitting behind a metal desk, punching figures into an adding machine. "Ellen! Is it really Ellen?"

We hugged hard. His hair had turned gray and his teeth were yellow, but he still looked fine. "You always had the best collarbones," I said into his neck. "How's Janine?"

"Fine, fine. Did you see my daughter out there? We finally had another daughter. She's on the junior varsity." When he smiled I saw that one of his darkening teeth had been capped and had a bluish cast.

We sat and passed the time for a few minutes. There was a map of a steer on the wall, each part labeled with the cuts of meat it provided. Reggie's daughter brought us coffee. I could see, now, how much she looked like Janine. The fact that there were no customers was misleading. Reggie said that he did mostly slaughtering, and business was good. "Janine's gotten fat as a house. You wouldn't believe it." He laughed appreciatively.

I was surprised to see that Reggie was no taller than I was. "Reggie, did you used to be taller, when you played basketball?"

He frowned. "I played guard."

"How's Cliff?"

"That shit. You can know somebody your whole life and not know anything about them."

. . .

Dinner at Bill Endicott's house began awkwardly. He was lonely, he said, and he'd burned the pork chops. Did I like opera?

His house, low-ceilinged and airless, was jumbled with broken antiques. "I don't know much about opera," I said, and he turned down the scratchy record he was playing. His stereo was of obviously poor quality, a weekend special from some discount house.

"Cliff loved it. He gave me this record. It's a rare recording. Very rare."

"Cliff from high school? That Cliff?"

He nodded, smiling. "Cliff died last year, you know."

"Cliff died?" I realized I was beginning to sound stupid. "I'm sorry. It's just that I saw Reggie today, and he didn't even tell me."

"Well, they grew apart."

Over his shoulder I saw a framed eight-by-ten photograph on an end table. Cliff's small, blinky eyes stared out of it. Mr. Endicott turned and picked it up and handed it to me.

I spoke carefully. "I didn't know."

"I worked for him some, Ellen, restoring furniture. Marla had a bad time, but I think she's all right now. She's a sweet girl."

"What did he die of?"

"Cancer."

We sat down at his kitchen dinette set. Its plastic wood contrasted with the faded antiques in the rest of the house. "Bill," I said, "did you know I'm gay too?"

He was pouring iced tea for us and hadn't heard.

"Bill," I said when he was looking at me, "I wanted you to know I'm gay."

Emotion rushed across his face. "Cliff told me."

"How . . ."

"He was an antique dealer, and he found out these things."

"Bill, did Cliff die of AIDS?"

"Of course not," he said too quickly, handing me the bowl of red rice. "Cliff was happily married. I worked for him. That was all."

I understood that he was lying to me. He'd probably made his decision to lie about Cliff long ago. I was sorry, because I would have liked for us to talk. "It's nice to see you again" was all I said.

He looked grateful, watching my lips. "It's nice to see you too, Ellen."

I tried to think of a question that wouldn't intrude. "How did you and Cliff get to know each other?"

He clutched his fork, and his faded eyes brightened. "In high school he used to write these notes on my blackboard. Do you remember the Phantom?"

I nodded and looked down, concentrating on cutting my pork chop.

"Well, he wrote me a very mean one and left something very mean on my doorstep. I won't say what. Then he came to my house to apologize, and we talked."

The pork chops really were burned. The red rice was flavorless, the broccoli frozen, served from a boiled plastic bag.

I smiled and looked Bill right in the eyes. "What a wonderful story," I said.

After dinner I lay sprawled on his sofa drinking cup after cup of instant coffee while he played me his scratchy opera records. He sat in a pink Victorian wing chair with his head tilted back, and once tears ran down his face. "Can you hear it?" he kept saying. "Can you hear it?"

"I hear it," I said.

Chapter 3

After my freshman year at Duke University, I went to summer school at Harvard. Because of the Boston Strangler, my mother didn't want me to go. "I just hate to *think* of you like that, with your face all purple and your tongue hanging out. Why can't you be a normal girl and get a tan?"

The dean at Duke probably wouldn't have wanted me to go to Harvard either. At Duke I was viewed as a troublemaker, partly because of hypnosis.

In high school I had learned how to hypnotize people by accident. "Look deep into my eyes," I said to my sister Marie one night, when we'd been watching an evil hypnotist in a B movie on television. I said this with great conviction, and Marie looked at me as if it were a joke. Then something peculiar happened: she seemed to drift toward my eyes. "I'm going to count to five," I whispered, "and when I get to five you'll be in a deep trance." I whispered because I was afraid. There was a current between us as certain as the electricity in a doorbell I'd once touched.

Marie's eyelids fluttered. As I counted to five, her eyes closed. "Can you bark?" I asked.

"Yes," she said.

"Will you do it?"

"Yes."

"Be a dog, then. Bark."

Her eyes remained closed, but Marie's lips pulled back from her teeth, and she began to make little yipping noises. I recognized our neighbor's chihuahua.

I counted backward from five and Marie woke up. "I don't think we ought to tell Momma or Aunt Doodles about this," I said.

During my senior year in high school I developed a different technique, no longer hypnotizing through eye contact, which scared me too much, but with a lighted cigarette in a semidark room. Making people bark remained my favorite trick. Sometimes I told them what kind of dog to be, and other times I allowed them to choose—German shepherd, Lhasa apso, whatever. I knew I shouldn't be doing hypnosis, especially at parties, but at Duke it made me popular and feared.

College caused me authority problems right from the beginning. There were rules against women wearing pants to classes or to the dining room, and rules against wearing curlers in public. There was even a "suggestion" that women shouldn't smoke cigarettes standing up. Soon there was a new regulation concerning hypnosis.

The Dean's summons came right after second semester began. For my audience I wore a madras wrap-around skirt, a Gant button-down shirt, and a cardigan that had leather patches on the elbows. I even wore a panty girdle and hose. She would see that I was a normal, healthy young woman, not a troublemaker.

Dean Pottle looked at least forty years old. Her hair was brown and she was wearing a brown tailored suit. Her skin revealed that she'd once had a mild case of acne. She was smoking a cigarette and seemed quite friendly as she invited me to sit down across from her.

"Ellen," she said comfortingly, "we have had a report that you went to Dr. Hillyer's class in the medical school wearing nothing but a bathing suit and carrying a bottle of champagne on a silver tray."

I tried to think of how best to reply. "I'm not in the medical school, Dean Pottle, so I didn't think the regular rules would apply. Anyway, it was Dr. Hillyer's birthday, and some of his students asked me to deliver the champagne. It seemed harmless enough. I would never have agreed to do it if I'd known the class was at eight-thirty in the morning, I can assure you of that."

When she said nothing, I elaborated. "I wore my trenchcoat over my bathing suit until I got to the door of the classroom, and I put it right back on as soon as I gave him the champagne."

Her eyes were less affable. "The same trenchcoat you've been wearing to your regular classes?"

I nodded.

"Is it true you've been wearing your trenchcoat to classes with nothing under it?"

"It certainly is not true, Dean Pottle. I wear a slip and a bra. I even wear hose."

"Ellen, you do know about the dress code, don't you?"

"I'm within the dress code, Dean Pottle. It just says you can't wear pants, it doesn't say you have to wear skirts. Also, a slip is a kind of skirt, isn't it?"

The Dean was trying to look stern, but I began to suspect she might like me. "Do you think of yourself as an unusual girl, Ellen?"

I nodded miserably. "Listen, Dean Pottle, would you mind if I smoked too? I'm pretty nervous."

"Go ahead. You have a tendency to bend the rules a bit, don't you think?"

I lit a Winston. "I don't know."

"Let's start with the hypnosis."

"There was no rule against hypnosis."

The Dean took a final meditative drag on her own cigarette and crushed it out in a brown glass ashtray.

"Anyway, there's not much to it," I said. "To hypnosis. I saw it on TV one night. I say corny stuff like 'Look only at the tip of my cigarette, your eyelids are getting heavy.' Most people are just dying to go into a trance."

The Dean was staring at the smoke curling slowly from my cigarette.

"Hello?" I said.

With effort she looked up at me. When she didn't speak, I continued. "I tell them, look at the glowing ember of the cigarette. Let your mind relax."

The Dean looked right back at my cigarette. She seemed

like a nice enough person. She probably thought the rules were dumb too.

"Your eyelids will close by themselves."

Her eyelids lowered quietly, like dancers bowing.

Slowly I counted to ten. "That's good. You're feeling very good. Just rest now."

A manila folder with my name on it was lying on her desk. In it were my college application, my board scores, and a handwritten report on the hypnosis incidents. The conclusion said I had difficulty accepting discipline and was on academic probation for poor grades.

I replaced the folder and said in my most soothing voice, "When you wake up, you'll feel great. You won't have any memory of this trance. No memory of it at all. You'll think Ellen Burns is a nice, interesting girl with no problems. Nod your head if you understand me."

The Dean nodded.

I was curious to know what kind of dog she might be, but someone could walk in and I wanted to put this unexpected opportunity to good use. Several acquaintances of mine were going to Harvard for the summer.

"When you wake up, I'm going to ask you about recommending me for summer school, and you're going to think that Harvard's a wonderful idea, in spite of my academic record. You'll say that Harvard is bound to help me with my authority problems. Do you understand?"

She nodded again.

I counted slowly backwards from ten to one, then said, "Wake up now."

The Dean's eyes opened. "I feel great. You're a wonderful girl, Ellen, with no serious problems."

I put out my cigarette in her brown glass ashtray. "Dean Pottle, I wanted to ask you about going to Harvard this summer."

I had made several unsuccessful attempts to lose my virginity at Duke, and Harvard had begun to seem like a possible solution.

My roommate at Duke was named Darlene. Darlene was an angular, good-looking girl with sharp cheekbones and black hair cut in a smooth pageboy that swayed when she moved.

She had been coaching me on the loss of my virginity. In high school I had read an article that said sperm could swim right through your underpants, so, whenever I got close to intercourse with a boy, I imagined microscopic tadpoles swimming desperately through cotton fibers the size of the columns at Stonehenge. And I was distracted by other thoughts: germs swim back and forth between mouths; the tongue is a muscle and disappears down the back of the throat, so what is it attached to?

"I want to be normal," I kept saying to Darlene. "I want to lose my normal virginity. Normally."

"I fixed you up with Don. He doesn't have any experience either. You can learn together."

"Darlene, how could that be a good idea?"

"Trust me, it's a good idea."

So Darlene arranged for this boy named Don to take me to dinner at a restaurant called Chicken in the Rough. The restaurant's logo was a long-legged chicken in a tam-o'-shanter swinging a golf club. Sitting in one of the dark red booths, I felt as if I were in a dentist's waiting room.

Don was melancholy, with dark, dramatic looks; his thick black eyebrows moved when he chewed. When he bit into a chicken leg I pointed at the tiny string of meat hanging from the bone. "That's a ligament, Don. In the fourth grade they told us that you could see what ligaments were when you ate fried chicken."

He looked uncertain.

"I only eat white meat," I said.

"Why are you telling me this?"

"Once the top of my mouth started getting loose. I could actually move the skin with my tongue. So I went to the dentist and said, 'The roof of my mouth is rotting off. I have some terrible disease.' He looked in my mouth and said, 'Do you eat soup?' So I said of course I eat soup. 'Do you drink coffee?' Yes, I drink coffee. 'Well, you're drinking it too hot.' I was kind of disappointed, you know? I thought I had some rare disease."

Don put down his chicken leg. "I don't know what Darlene said to you, but we don't have to do anything. We really don't."

"Could we drink some beer?" I said.

So, while the chicken and fried potatoes congealed in their grease and the salad wilted in its pool of dressing, Don and I drank a pitcher of beer, and I began to relax. Don was a good enough looking boy, although he lacked the wildness I found compelling in Darlene's boyfriend, who had taken the mike away from the singer of a black blues band at a fraternity party and sung an original version of "Put Your Head on My Shoulder" called "Put Your Legs Round My Shoulders."

Don had been raised by his grandmother in Greensboro, North Carolina. When he graduated he wanted to be a newspaper reporter in a small Southern town. He said his grandmother's lifelong wish was to meet Lawrence Welk. Someday Don hoped to arrange that for her.

"I have to go to the bathroom," I said.

In the bathroom I confronted the most serious obstacle to the loss of my virginity: Under my skirt I was wearing a panty girdle. I hadn't really meant to wear the girdle, but when I was dressing I kept hearing my mother's voice saying, *Any woman looks better in a girdle,* so I'd put it on experimentally, and it felt so secure, so bracing, that I'd left it on. Now I didn't know what to do about it. I considered taking it off, but it was too bulky for the pocket of my trenchcoat.

What I did have in the pocket of my trenchcoat was a Norform vaginal suppository that Darlene had given me to insert "just before intercourse." It was supposed to lubricate me, a word that made me feel like a car. But when was "just before intercourse"? After I peed, I inserted the suppository and pulled the girdle back into place, feeling deeply relieved. The girdle meant I couldn't make love, but the suppository meant I sincerely wanted to.

On the way out of Chicken in the Rough I stopped at the

bar in the front room and downed a double shot of bourbon, neat. "I never met anybody like you," Don said.

"I'm absolutely normal," I said, feeling a rush of love for the shot glass. "I'm normal for me. Really."

The November night was inky blue, the air clean and brisk. Don put his arm around me as we walked. The bourbon warmed my blood and the melting Norform made me feel odd. I stopped Don on the street and kissed him on the mouth the way I thought someone in a movie might kiss.

Soon we were in the dormitory parking lot, leaning against a stranger's empty car, still kissing cinematically. Then we were in the back seat of the same car, half lying down. Just when the kissing was getting boring, Don put his hand up my skirt. I had never had anyone's hand up my skirt before.

His fingers moved tentatively up my legs. "My god, what's this?" he said, encountering the girdle.

I wanted to explain but I was too dizzy.

His hand wandered around the flesh of my thigh, then moved inward and upward. The dissolved Norform was all over the crotch of the girdle. "My god, you're wet," he said.

I tried to hold still.

"Okay," he mumbled, sliding two fingers awkwardly up the leg of the panty girdle. When he touched me something flashed in my head, and my hips pushed hard against his hand.

"Oh my god, oh my god," he said, pulling his hand free.

"I'll take it off," I said. "No problem. Here, I can take it off."

Don was still crouched over his hand. His fingers glistened

in the darkness. A lump appeared behind his knuckle and swelled while I watched.

"It's . . . it's growing," I said.

"It's sprained," he said.

I became famous almost overnight.

Don told no one about the girdle, but he did admit to Darlene's boyfriend that his injury was "sort of sexual."

"Sort of sexual," Darlene's boyfriend said. "What is *sort of* sexual?"

Don's hand was not sprained. He had broken a blood vessel behind his knuckle. Overnight the blood spread under his skin, turning it puffy and greenish. By the end of the week his hand had turned black, with a dark red palm.

Boys I'd never heard of called me at the dorm, and Don followed me to several classes. "We'll try it again. We've got to try it again." He looked vulnerable, stunned by love, extending his black hand.

I never wanted to see Don again in my whole life, so I felt relieved when my mother telephoned and said, "Why don't you fly home this weekend and get measured for your hand-sewn human-hair wig?"

She met me at the airport in Charleston, just before midnight on a Friday. She was wearing purple toreador pants, a gold lamé shirt, gold lamé slippers, a stroller-length mink coat, and large dark glasses. "I don't want anyone to *recognize* me," she whispered, looking uneasily around the deserted airport. "That's why I have on these *glasses.*"

For a year my mother had been addicted to diet pills. *"Am-bars,"* she would say in a singsongy voice. "I was a different person before I found *Am-bars!* The *am* stands for amphetamine and the *bar* stands for barbiturate! The amphetamine speeds you *up,* and the barbiturate slows you down. You don't have any appetite, but you're not *ner*vous!"

Before my mother found diet pills, she did not speak in italics and exclamations, and she was not wiry and loud. Before she found diet pills, she was heavy and depressed. Now she liked to scrub the tiles in the bathroom with a toothbrush, and she had fired the maid because she said it felt so good to push the vacuum cleaner around and polish the silverware herself. She liked to get down between the tines of the forks. "It takes *patience,"* she said. "I have *lots* of patience!"

Her arms vibrated as she embraced me. "Doesn't it look real?" she whispered. "Isn't it *astounding?"* She patted her French twist.

Her hair was so smoothly arranged that no false scalp showed, but the elegant twist looked odd: My mother's real hair is naturally curly.

The next day I was staring at myself in the beautician's mirror. "Thank you, Momma." Like Momma's wig, Aunt Doodles's wig, and my sister Marie's wig, my wig was set in a French twist.

The four of us were standing around the beauty parlor. We had the monolithic look of a gang. "The French Twist gang," Marie said quietly, meeting my eyes in the mirror. Marie had grown tall and fragile, a natural blond with a sweet smile and a quiet manner. She was three years younger than me.

Aunt Doodles was married to my mother's brother Royce, for whom my little brother Royce had been named. "We all look alike in these wigs," Doodles said, "but I'm the inflated version." Doodles didn't care for the diet pills because she said they made her heart hurt.

Doodles was built square, "like a refrigerator," she would announce cheerfully. She wheezed loudly almost all of the time. "There's just not much room for air in there," Marie had once remarked.

After my wig fitting, we went shopping, and I bought a garter belt. "I'm not wearing girdles anymore, Momma. Don't ask. I'm just not, no matter what."

The wig not only changed how I looked, it changed how I felt about myself. When I got back to school, boys stopped pursuing me. Perhaps they no longer recognized the black hand girl. I abandoned not only hypnosis but parties, and my study habits improved. By the time I got to Harvard, I had been taken off academic probation. Dean Pottle later claimed that her confidence in me had "turned me around."

I met Nicky Sommers on a sticky Saturday night in a drugstore in Harvard Square, where I was buying a new copy of *Peyton Place* because the pages of my copy were falling out. He was buying a book called *Thinking about the Unthinkable,* which I assumed was pornographic but turned out to be about nuclear war.

My copy of *Peyton Place* was worn-out because, in the long afternoons in my apartment in Back Bay, while my room-mate, Dottie Plant, was out waitressing, I had discovered masturbation.

When I was wearing the wig I dressed like a Duke sorority girl and studied calmly, but when I was not wearing the wig a certain wildness seemed to overtake me. "Anything goes," I sang one night and danced around the apartment as if I were in a musical comedy. So I tried to wear my French twist almost every day, and I was making very good grades. Dean Pottle was going to be proud.

My wig got gummy with dirt, and I had to give it up for six days to have it professionally cleaned. Without the wig I began to wear white lipstick. I combed my hair out straight and drank scotch on the rocks while I studied. Sometimes I dressed in a black jersey and tight black jeans and imagined I was a beatnik like the ones I'd seen in *Time* magazine. I was in Cambridge, Massachusetts, I reasoned, and no one in North or South Carolina need ever know I was behaving this way.

Sexually, I began to experiment. I read the sex scenes in *Peyton Place* and drifted into them like hypnosis, my old teddy bear clutched tight between my legs. I felt bad about my teddy bear, who was not holding up well under this assault, but as long as I didn't touch myself, I was sure I couldn't be doing anything wrong. Then, one afternoon when it was too hot in the apartment to wear a lot of clothes, my wildness overcame my scruples. I bled and it wasn't my period. As the word *masturbation* occurred to me, I realized I had deflowered myself.

My wig would be available on Monday. On Saturday night, since I was ruined anyway, I went to a drugstore in Harvard Square in my white lipstick, black jersey and tight black jeans, to buy a new copy of *Peyton Place*. I was standing furtively behind the paperback rack when this boy wearing Levi's that looked as if they hadn't been washed in two weeks said, "Are you from down home?" He had an unmistakable Southern drawl.

I didn't answer, of course, or even look up. My mother's warnings about the Boston Strangler had made a vivid impression on me, so vivid, in fact, that when I tried to swear off *Peyton Place,* long fantasies about the Boston Strangler had drifted in to replace it.

"Southerners look different," he continued. "We walk different, or something."

That the Boston Strangler was a Southerner seemed unlikely, so I looked him full in the face. "Where are you from?"

"Texas." He had a nice smile but crooked teeth. His hair was stringy, and he wore glasses.

"Texas isn't the South," I said. "Texas is the West."

If I hadn't agreed to go drink beer with Nicky Sommers, I wouldn't have told him funny stories about my family, and if he hadn't laughed so much at these stories I wouldn't have drunk so much. If I hadn't drunk so much I wouldn't have ended up back at my apartment with him, and if Dottie Plant had been home I wouldn't have ended up on the sofa with him. If he hadn't been lying with his skinny hip jammed against my tight black jeans, I wouldn't have drifted into *Peyton Place.*

Your nipples are as hard as diamonds, the irresistible man whispered.

Do it to me, the woman whispered back.

Nicky unbuttoned my shirt and cupped his hand over my breast.

"Diamonds!" I shouted, and we both began to shudder. I was extremely embarrassed and kept my eyes shut tight.

"Hey," he kept saying, "hey," but not as if he expected any response.

I was breathing as if I'd been running.

"Wow," Nicky whispered, "you had an orgasm."

"I certainly did not." I was trying not to cry.

"Wow. I never gave a girl an orgasm. Hey. Wow."

When Nicky arrived at my apartment for our first real date the next Monday night, he had cut his hair and shaved so close his jaw looked raw and scraped. We were going to dinner at a French restaurant where, he promised, the menu would be written in French.

Nicky was wearing a suit and tie, and on his feet were grown-up, lace-up men's shoes. In his hand was a bouquet of daisies.

I had picked up my wig from the cleaners. I was wearing a blue sheath dress, my garter belt, hose, and high heels.

"Your hair looks great that way," Nicky said.

We stared dumbly at each other, like people who have fallen in love.

Chapter 4

Uncle Royce smoked cigars. Sometimes he didn't bother to light them but chewed the ends so thoroughly they seemed to have exploded behind his teeth. When he wasn't mauling the cigars, he was stuffing his lower lip with fat wads of tobacco that he pulled from a Red Man envelope. When I was a child Uncle Royce would yell "Duck!" and spit on me before I could move. The raw stain appeared on my face, my shirt.

Uncle Royce was often our babysitter. Scooter and Sally and Diggs were his own children; my sister and little brother and I were outsiders. When Marie was still a baby, Uncle Royce would rock her carefully while he told us tales of Greylocks, the monster who lived in closets and under beds. If I got too close to my uncle, he pinched me hard enough to bruise.

Uncle Royce worked at the post office in downtown Charleston. My father had his own business, but our families spent a lot of time together. My parents had trouble conceiving children, so, for a while, until I was born, it was as if Sally and Diggs had two sets of parents.

Uncle Royce told me I was the ugliest baby he'd ever seen. He said I looked like a dry, shriveled apple. My mother said Uncle Royce loved children. He loved the fears of children. He loved my fears.

About him I still have partial amnesia. I remember that on Sundays he would pick us up after church in his station wagon and take us to Griswold Park. We each got a box of Cracker Jacks. I studied the prizes inside, puzzled that they weren't any better. We fed the swans stale bread. The swans were mean and elegant, gliding eerily, like dreams.

In summers he drove us to the lake house, stopping along the way to buy us Cokes and little bags of peanuts out of vending machines. I liked to pour the salty peanuts right into the Coke bottle and then suck them back through the narrow neck.

Once, when Uncle Royce got drunk and came home late, Aunt Doodles opened their front door and shouted, "Why'd you bother to come home?" Uncle Royce smiled, wavering hugely, and said, "I came home to see my little Doo-Dolls."

I know Uncle Royce loved cows. In the winter we would sometimes go for a weekend to visit our grandmother's farm. Our grandmother was a tall, gray-haired lady who baked biscuits for breakfast. The honey had wax combs in it, and the milk was warm, dipped from a pail. One morning I watched Uncle Royce milking the cow. He touched her carefully.

Uncle Royce was always pulling my pants down to expose

my buttocks. "I see the moon rise," he'd say. Only a foolish child got near him with her back turned, or forgot and sat behind him when he was driving. The tobacco spitting was legitimate then. He yelled "Duck!" and spit, and the juice flew back through the window, and Aunt Doodles or my mother said, "Royce!"

I was six or seven years old when he put a wooden clothes-pin on the soft underside of my arm, bruising me badly. Maddened by pain, I crossed the room, made my arms into a battering ram with my fists locked together, and hit him at full speed. I nearly knocked him down. My mother spanked me. "You hurt him," she said. "You hurt your Uncle Royce."

My father wasn't with us. He was tied up at work. I couldn't understand how he knew when they were going to untie him.

When I was in high school, we moved to the country, and my father went to work one day and didn't come home. I didn't get to say goodbye. I couldn't remember what I had for breakfast that morning or even if we were in the kitchen at the same time.

At the funeral the casket was open at first, but then they closed it, and I started thinking, *What if he's not really in there?*

After the funeral my little brother sat on the floor of the living room playing with Lincoln Logs. He made a brown log cabin with a green roof and a red chimney. "Daddy's dead," he said over and over, smiling.

Uncle Royce liked to play a game with his dog: he would try to hit it with the car when he drove into the yard. We all shrieked as the dog disappeared under the wheels. Miraculously, when we looked behind us, the dog would still be chasing the car.

One Sunday, soon after my father was buried, there was a nauseating thud, the sound of flesh hitting hard. Uncle Royce stopped the car, and we all stood around in our Sunday School clothes, looking at the dog. It was bleeding from the mouth, staring at Uncle Royce. He made us walk on up to the house. Later my mother said, "Royce feels terrible over his dog."

"He hit it on purpose."

"Don't be silly," she said. "Royce loved his dog."

By the time I was fifteen, the dark was full of nightmares, and I took tranquilizers to sleep. At breakfast I was so stupid that more than once I embarrassed myself by sticking my fork into my cheek, missing my mouth.

I didn't have a boyfriend, except for Scott, who was shorter than I was and a year younger. Scott was femininely graceful and a good dancer. We saw *La Dolce Vita* together four times and called each other Maddalena and Marcello. In nightclubs that shouldn't have admitted us we danced, wearing our dark glasses. Outside, in parking lots, we drank martinis from a glass jar and gave each other worldly looks. "I can't tell cruelty from love," I'd say.

Marie stayed pretty through adolescence, but she was sick a lot. She could bring our mother and me out of our stupors by stopping breathing. There was an oxygen tank in Marie's bedroom, and asthma inhalers were scattered around the house. Once, when I had taken her to the hospital and she was lying in one of those emergency-room cubicles gasping like a guppy that had jumped out of our aquarium, I leaned over her and whispered, "Did Uncle Royce do something bad to you when you were little?"

Marie's brown eyes were frightened, her blond hair damp with sweat. She was too sick to speak.

"Did he do mean things to you?"

The doctor had come in behind me, but I couldn't stop. "Did he burn you with his cigar? Did he touch you really hard?"

In college my family history seemed to recede. I got interested in civil rights, astronomy, and partying. During the day I thought about social injustice, and at night, drunk, I looked up through the ceiling at the stars.

The man I married liked to touch me, which made me feel ashamed. Shame excited me. Nicky was a scientist who did volunteer work for the civil rights movement. He was no one dramatic. When we made love I saw rows of numbers rising over his shoulders through the roof, curving toward infinity.

I liked being married to Nicky, liked the sound of his breathing and the feel of his warm body in bed at night, but his personality stayed as smooth and impervious to me as a stone. He told our marriage counselor that I was inaccessible, an accusation that seemed misplaced.

Several years after our divorce, I went for a weekend to an ashram in upstate New York. My drinking was getting out of control, and I had developed an inner-ear disorder diagnosed as psychosomatic. An old friend of mine from college had told me about an Indian guru who'd helped her in some way she couldn't explain. "Maybe Rama's a shyster, or maybe he's not. If he is, he's a hell of a good one."

The ashram was in a converted hotel in the Catskills. Statues of Einstein, Martin Luther King, Jesus, and the Virgin Mary were arranged across the lawn. "These are the people Rama likes," a guide told me. It all seemed so hokey I felt quite safe, but the first time I saw Rama I fell to my knees, which surprised me greatly—I wasn't raised a Catholic—and I began crying, which also surprised me. As an adult, I have not been much of a crier.

"I've come here about my balance," I murmured. Rama, who was wearing an orange silk robe, was sitting cross-legged on a kind of throne. I felt especially silly since he didn't speak English. He worked through an interpreter, who, on this occasion, didn't bother to translate my remark.

Rama looked bored as he tapped me with a peacock feather. I didn't have much of a response to this feather business, but later, when the crowd—there were hundreds of people, maybe a thousand, in the converted ballroom—began to chant a mantra, I started shivering from the beauty of the sound.

The next day Rama stopped me in the hallway as if I were a passing thought. With his palm he struck me sharply on the forehead. For a few seconds I saw a blue light so lovely I felt willing to spend the rest of my life trying to see it again.

I stayed quietly in the ashram for six weeks, using up my sick leave and my paid vacation. I didn't drink at all, and I

held still a great deal. I slept in a dormitory-style room with
five other women. At night I lay awake, listening to us
breathing.

Not all of my inner traveling was pleasant. Sometimes
awful noises came out of my mouth in the meditation room,
which could sound like a ward for the dying. Karma cleaning, Rama called it, the light of God burning away our per-
sonal histories. I began to see the blue light often, and within
it a tiny white pearl, an unwinking point of light that Rama
said was my individual soul.

Once, during meditation, I began to drift toward a huge
black sun with an orange corona. As I neared it, I moved
faster and faster. At the last minute I realized it was not a
black sun but the pupil of an enormous eye, and I shot
through it into outer space. I was flying through stars when
I thought, *This is real,* and immediately woke up.

"A very high experience," Rama said when I told him
about it through his interpreter. "You have passed through
the eye of God."

The interpreter was a former professor who had special-
ized in Hindu religions before finding, as he put it, the deep
end of the pool. He had a narrow face and was losing his
hair. His expression as he translated was peculiar, and I
wondered if he was jealous.

I was living in Boston at the time, and when I got back to
my apartment I set up a little altar to Rama in my bedroom
closet. I soon lost interest in meditation and began drinking
again, though, for a while, not as heavily. I continued to see
the blue light sometimes, out of the corner of my eye or as

I was falling asleep, but I felt contented enough with my work and my life. My balance problem was gone.

I was working as a book editor and handling several good minor writers; mostly I oversaw projects that generated income, like *Japanese Gardening in a New England Setting* or *The Ninety-Second Diet.* I liked my job and made a decent living at it.

"I'm achieving normalcy in some areas of my life," I told my sister when she came to visit.

I hadn't seen Marie in several years. She came alone, although by now she had a husband and two children. This was her first time North and her first time away from them, and I sensed that she wanted something from me she couldn't articulate.

Although her blond hair had darkened to brown and she was twenty pounds overweight, Marie looked as beautiful to me as ever. We did some sightseeing—a visit to Faneuil Hall, a dinner at Durgin Park—but mostly we sat in my Back Bay apartment and drank gin.

"I have a normal life, too," she told me more than once, only she said this as if hers were some kind of joke. She said my face looked "easier." I did imitations of the guru and his translator and described the ashram in detail, and we laughed a lot.

She brought me the family news. Aunt Doodles had had a fibroid tumor the size of a cantaloupe removed; Doodles's doctor had taken a color photograph of the tumor, which she enjoyed showing around. "Maybe she'll put it on her Christmas card," Marie said. Cousin Sally had figured out what to do about the Christmas tree: she'd wrapped it in Saran Wrap so she could leave it up year round. "Thank God for artificial trees," Sally had said. "This would never have been possible with the living ones."

Uncle Royce had killed another dog. The dog pound had shown on TV a Doberman pinscher that was so vicious it was being put to sleep. Somehow Uncle Royce got possession of this dog. He penned it up and starved it for six weeks, until it was obedient and dependent on him. The dog growled at everyone else. My sister didn't let her sons near the dog, or near Uncle Royce either.

"But Uncle Royce *loves* children!" we said in unison. We were standing in the kitchen, and we laughed so hard we had to hold each other up.

My sister wiped away her tears and drained her gin and tonic. "Momma thinks you're so different since you left, but you're the same."

"No," I said, "I'm not the same."

"I wish you lived nearer home."

Uncle Royce had been asleep on the front-porch divan when his new dog attacked him. "It tore his arm *up,*" Marie said, and we giggled. "Seventeen stitches!" We kept laughing.

"He hung it," she said suddenly, and now the tears were not from laughter. "My sons saw him do it." She got out her inhaler.

"We've had too much gin, Marie. I wish I weren't drinking again."

"You just look so much easier," she said, wheezing. "In your face."

Soon after Marie's visit, my mother telephoned me. Even during her Episcopalian years my mother was secretly a Baptist. Now she was going through a brief extremist phase. I thought maybe she had a crush on her minister.

My mother had heard from Marie about the ashram, and she was certain I was going to hell. "Don't *worry* about it," I told her. She argued fiercely about vegetarianism. "It's not *normal.* Did it occur to you, when you were in that place, that they could've been drugging your food?"

"Momma," I kept saying, "I'm not a vegetarian."

Two months after visiting me, Marie dropped dead in a grocery store. "She couldn't breathe," said the clerk who gave her mouth-to-mouth resuscitation. "She had an inhaler but it didn't help her." The inhaler didn't help because Marie was having a heart attack. I hated thinking of her trying to breathe, a stranger's mouth locked over hers, forcing his air down her throat.

Rama's followers do not wear any special clothing, but I went to Marie's funeral wearing bright red silk, as if I were a follower of the notorious guru Rajneesh. I wasn't sure my mother would know about Rajneesh, although he'd been on TV a lot, so I painted a red dot on my forehead.

My mother grabbed me by the wrist at the funeral home. "How can you do this to your sister? How can you do this to me?"

"Do what?" I said.

"You've always been wicked, and now you're going straight to hell."

My sister's sons, who were six and four, were holding my hands. At their age no one looks strange. "She's a nun," Toby, the six-year-old, said.

"Catholics," my mother said. "The very worst."

The boys and I went to gaze at a tank of tropical fish in the receiving room. The room smelled of air fresheners. "Did your mother tell you I was a nun?" I asked Toby.

He was tracing across the glass of the aquarium the path of a fish with a red dot on its stomach. He nodded without looking up.

"I'm not a nun, honey," I said. "I'm not even a careful person."

I took the boys into the church and we sat in the pew beside their father. Keith was a kind man, and I felt grateful to him for letting the children be with me this way. Despite my outfit and the dot on my forehead, I thought he could see Marie in my face.

Uncle Royce was one of the pallbearers. He limped. He'd gotten fat and old. The doctors had told him that if he didn't quit drinking he'd die, and without alcohol he looked timid and uncertain.

Just before the service, I whispered to Toby, "Are you afraid of Uncle Royce?" Keith, whom everyone called Kit, was clutching my red silk.

"He's bad," Toby whispered back, and Kit nodded, echoing "bad" loud enough to make my mother lean forward in the pew and glare.

The ceremony was sanctimonious and crude. My mother's minister was a blustering glad-hander who radiated falseness and called my sister saved. Marie had not even believed in God.

Near the end of the service, a woman stepped from behind a curtain and, accompanied by canned backup music, sang a love song about Jesus.

I was breathing hard when Toby whispered, "Are you sick?"

I felt dizzy and confused. Then a voice inside me said *angry*. "Angry," I said out loud. My mother leaned over and slapped my arm, as if I were a child.

When I got back home to Boston, I tried to take up meditation again, but I had gone black inside where the blue light had been, and when my inner screen finally lit back up, what I saw was ghastly: black horses vomiting blackness; a silver knife protruding from my navel; a cave full of snakes that I was chloroforming one by one while I joked, *This will make a great living room.* Twice I woke up from the meditation gagging.

I went back to the ashram and asked for a private audience with Rama. I told him about my sister and my uncle. "I know he did something terrible to us, Rama, but I can't remember. I think I'm full of hate, but I can't feel it." The interpreter was enjoying this translation.

"Ah, yes, hate," Rama said. "You must go to your uncle and make amends to him."

"Make amends to him? Rama, that can't be right."

"Your hatred is your enemy," Rama said, "not your uncle. You must make amends for your hatred for your own sake." The interpreter was grinning, showing stained, uneven teeth.

I wish I'd done something dramatic, such as hitting Rama with his own peacock feather, but I merely brooded about his advice overnight. "I can't accept what you said."

Rama seemed unsurprised. "I'll miss you." Even gurus make jokes.

Uncle Royce picked me up at the airport. My mother was busy having a manicure from a Korean woman. "Those Orientals are so smart, honey," she told me over the phone. "They're going to take over the whole U.S. of A. I'm glad you're coming home."

"I'm just coming for a visit."

Uncle Royce was driving his old white Cadillac, which looked like a movie prop. He was chewing a cigar.

I put my own bags in the trunk. He was still huge but seemed weak.

As we pulled away from the curb I said, "How many miles you got on this thing?" The interior of the car smelled strongly of tobacco. A pack of Red Man was on the seat.

"One forty," he said, spitting thick black juice into a Coke bottle.

"I remember when you used to try to get us to drink out of those Coke bottles."

He nodded almost imperceptibly.

"I remember a lot of things."

We drove in silence to the house.

My mother had moved in with Uncle Royce and Aunt Doodles, and Cousin Sally still lived at home. Her married brothers often brought their families over. They lived in a fifties copy of a plantation house, complete with columns. Scooter, as soon as he was rich, had bought this house for his parents. There were formal rooms no one used, a massive living room, a dining room, a study. Everyone hung out in the family room and the kitchen, which were chaotic and messy. A television played continually, and almost every night a card game formed around the kitchen table.

The adults liked to play a game called "Go to Hell." I remembered this game vaguely from high school, and on the first night I sat by Uncle Royce and won.

During a break I sliced a pepperoni.

"I thought you were a vegetarian," my mother said, studying her new acrylic nails.

"I told you I'm not a vegetarian," I said.

I was supposed to sleep upstairs in one of the bedrooms, but the windows were painted shut and I felt claustrophobic, so I went downstairs and stretched out on a sofa in the family room. I lay awake watching the stream of cool air from the vent move the heavy curtains. My anger seemed gone, my uncle pathetic, the deflated figure of a nightmare.

I awoke to the sound of my mother crying.

She sat across the room from me in the dim light at the

kitchen table. She was wearing a blue nightgown with Coca-Cola written across the back of it. Her head, helmeted by a hairnet, rested forehead down on the blond wood table. "It's too hard," she was saying. "It's too hard."

I went over and sat beside her. I didn't know what else to do.

"Marie's dead, and your brother won't even come home for the funeral. And you don't even live here anymore."

The pores in her cheeks were waxy and bluish without makeup. When I tried to put my arm around her, she shoved me away. "Oh god, Ellen Larraine, it really is too hard."

I put my arm back around her, and then she turned and embraced me.

"Ellen Larraine," I said out loud. No one had called me by both my names since I was a child.

We sat that way for maybe half a minute. Then I said, "Momma, do you know what Uncle Royce did to Marie and me when we were little?"

She pulled away and the light caught her artificial nails. "What do you mean?"

"Do you know what Uncle Royce did to Marie and me when we were little? I know he did something."

"Uncle Royce loves you."

"Momma, this really matters."

She peeled the acrylic nail off her thumb, exposing a pink, bitten nub.

"Momma."

Bright blood formed at the base of her nail. "He burned you," she said.

I tried to keep my breathing even. "How did he burn me?"

"With matches."

"Where?"

"In your navel. With a match. I caught him. I don't know what else."

"What about Marie?"

She peeled open the other thumb, which bled too. "I don't know. Isn't that enough?"

"Why did you let him?"

"I don't know . . . scared. Honey, he was my brother."

"Me too. I was scared too."

I stroked her shoulder, and after a while I took her back up to bed. She let me tuck the sheets around her and kiss her cheek, which smelled of cold cream. She looked frail and old. "It's all my fault, Ellen Larraine. It's my fault, isn't it?"

"No one's fault," I said, though I wasn't sure.

For the rest of the night I lay awake on the sofa, burning. Matches flared in my mind and were extinguished. I smelled sulfur. There were other memories I will not name. Sometimes I heard my own voice screaming, and sometimes I heard Marie's. I tried to hold Marie's face before me. "I'm listening," I kept saying out loud. "I hear you, Marie." I stuffed a pillow between my legs to help the pain.

In the morning, for breakfast, Aunt Doodles made blueberry pancakes. She heated Aunt Jemima syrup, and we all sat around the blond wood table.

My mother had bandaged her thumbs. She seemed afraid

74

to look at me, but I felt oddly okay. I even made a joke to Uncle Royce, my favorite joke from childhood. "What's green and has wheels?"

He shook his head.

"Grass," I said. "I was just kidding about the wheels."

Later, because it was Saturday and there was a new mall, we all went shopping. The mall had two stories and was very long, with escalators at each end. Cathedral ceilings made it seem like a kind of church. I imagined the mall filled with the sound of Rama's followers chanting.

Momma held on to my arm as if she were a child. "This must seem strange as the moon for you," she said.

"I live in Boston, Momma. They have malls in Boston."

She squeezed my elbow. "I mean strange to be home."

"Yes, it's strange to be home."

"Would you let me come visit you?"

"Of course."

She bought clothes for me, serviceable cotton pants and sweaters. "I wish Marie was here," she said.

"I do too."

For the last few years Aunt Doodle's arteries had hardened and she'd become increasingly anxious outside her house, so as we explored the mall, she stayed close to my mother. Uncle Royce, unsteady on his feet, followed Doodles. He sat outside each store on the benches by the ashtrays, chewing his cigar. Diggs and his wife and their daughters went off by themselves. We'd arranged to meet them at the cafeteria upstairs for lunch.

Riding the escalator to the cafeteria, I felt, through the

metal steps, an expected jolt. "Royce!" I heard Doodles shout.

I looked behind me. Uncle Royce had tripped and fallen. He was on his hands and knees, a cigar still stuck in his mouth. The escalator continued to move, and he couldn't stand back up.

For several seconds we rode that way, our eyes fastened on each other. I wish I could say some kind of acknowledgment passed between us.

The escalator stopped, and a harsh alarm sounded. Two security guards were running toward us.

"Oh no, oh no!" Doodles shouted.

My mother wailed once, "Royce!"

I crossed the few steps separating Uncle Royce from me and stooped down beside him. A few strands of gray hair hung across his wide, emotionless face. I put my hand carefully on his shoulder. "Don't be afraid," I said.

Chapter 5

The year my father was killed, our family had just moved to an old plantation out in the country. Before we moved to Blacklock, we lived in a little house on the outskirts of Charleston. In our old neighborhood, there was a house identical to ours on every street. I had never seen a house like the one at Blacklock, except in the movies.

But Blacklock wasn't much like Tara. Each time *Gone With the Wind* was rereleased, our family, minus my father, went dutifully to see this tribute to what we had lost. When "Dixie" played (the boy with the flute had just found out his brother was dead and he had tears in his eyes), I cried every time. And when Scarlett O'Hara said, "As God is my witness, I'll never be hungry again," I'd think, *yeah, me either.* We were minus my father because he was tied up making money, and he was making money so we could do things like move to Blacklock.

My father had grown up poor. His father had been a bootlegger, but I wasn't told that particular detail until much later—on my wedding day by my Aunt Doodles, who took off her gloves and had two drinks. Like my brother and sister, I was raised on the myth of our father's childhood, as presented by my mother: he had grown up in a house without glass in the windows; for Christmas he got his sister's old crayons, or a few firecrackers to throw at the chickens. He was the only child in his family to graduate from high school; unable to afford the books, he finished anyway. My mother, I found out much later, had also grown up deprived, but women, she believed, could not be self-made. A man was whatever he set out to be, she instructed me, but a woman was whatever she was born.

The main house at Blacklock was a large frame structure with a porch that wrapped around it on three sides. Set on a slight rise, it had nevertheless been built up off the ground, because of the proximity of the river. The original house presumably had burned. When workmen from my father's business walled in the foundation, they found wooden pins instead of nails, which dated the place to the seventeenth century. They also found twenty-four snakes beneath the house. These were mostly black snakes and king snakes, good ones, my father said, except for the two rattlers, but I think my uneasiness began then. There were times, even before my father was killed, when I felt something cold and black and slick moving beneath me, something walled in and forgotten.

Or maybe my uneasiness began the first time we drove out to "the farm"—as we called Blacklock, to show our modesty, and because it didn't look like Tara. My daddy's new two-tone blue Ford moved slowly through scrub woods and marshes, country as flat as the desert in the movies, but not empty like the desert. The road to Blacklock was crowded with live oaks that hung over it and black people who walked sullenly along its edges. Tucked into the open spaces were wooden shacks, trailers, and small cinderblock buildings. Steam rose off the pavement, and the air felt too close.

We turned off the paved road through old gray-white posts that had once held a gate, and now the moss-draped oaks joined over the dirt road, creating a tunnel. The shacks here were even closer to the road. I saw an old woman chewing a corncob pipe. A man in denim coveralls that were faded almost white nodded as if we were friends. A teenage boy glanced at us with what I knew instinctively was hate. "These were the old slave cabins," my mother said.

Then we passed through a set of white stone columns with a green wooden gate and moved slowly up a white oyster-shell road that circled in front of the house on top of the hill. A huge oak whose branches brushed the ground dominated the "yard," some two acres of thick grass scattered with pecan and pear trees. Beyond the fence were twenty acres of pasture, complete with cattle. Behind the house, at the bottom of the hill, stretched fifty acres of old rice paddies, flooded now with salt water and ruined. They were beautiful, the graceful marsh grass crisscrossed by small, glittering canals.

But I kept staring at the house, wondering if it was the shutters, maybe, or the peeling paint that made it seem sinister. "I've seen this movie before," I said to my father, but he didn't pay any attention. "I've seen this movie before!" I shouted.

"Hush, Ellen," my father said.

I was at a melodramatic age. One of my favorite tricks was to crawl down the hallway of our house in the suburbs whimpering, "As God is my witness, I'll never, never, never, never . . ." I could actually get tears in my eyes doing this, and my mother would laugh so hard. "Oh, Tallulah," she'd say, as if to the actress Tallulah Bankhead. I liked my mother a lot, but I thought it would be terrible to be named Bankhead. My name was Ellen Larraine, after my grandmother, the one who'd lived in the house without any glass in the windows. I liked my name so much I wrote it everywhere, and already I was fingering the pencil in my pocket, wondering where I could write my name on this house so that no one would find it.

My dad had the keys and we walked through the empty house, making plans. There was a living room forty feet long, with a double fireplace angling out into the middle of it. My mother spoke of the two chandeliers that would hang at either end, the burgundy velvet drapes that would grace the windows, how the old wide boards of the pine floor would be refinished till they glowed. She would get Victorian sofas for opposite ends of the living room, and a piano for my sister.

Upstairs my brother and sister and I were each allotted a bedroom; the fourth would be for our parents. There was only one bathroom upstairs and it would have to be remodeled. There would be twin bathrooms, my mother said, with square tubs; maybe she would paint them a very pale pink and a very pale blue.

My mother was happy before we moved to Blacklock, or at least that is how I remember her. At the house in Riverland Terrace we had baked cakes together, and she let me make seven-minute frosting myself, emptying the mix into a deep metal bowl and running the electric mixer. Afterwards we each licked one of the beaters. You can do anything you want to do, my mother would tell me, if you just believe in yourself enough. She seemed to be forgetting, at these moments, her view about the limitations of females, or perhaps forgetting my gender.

My mother was tall and dark-haired and she had brown, deep-set eyes, just like mine. Her laugh seemed to come from a rich, secret place.

I don't remember much about my father from these years, except that when I was little he taught me to play marbles. No child of mine is going to lose at marbles, he said, and we went into the backyard and he drew a circle in the dirt. It's mental, he told me. I was six years old. Don't aim. Think your way through the marble. Imagine yourself hitting it.

I thought my father was handsome. He was wearing an undershirt and he had big muscles. His dark hair was slicked back. He had brown, deep-set eyes, just like mine.

The day we moved to the farm there was a fierce lightning storm. The moving van was parked in the oyster-shell circle, and the moving men huddled on the porch. My mother had invited them into the house but they wouldn't come. Lightning struck near the house several times. I didn't know anything could be so loud or so near and not hurt me. I stood in what would become the family room and stared out the window at the huge oak. A sheet of water seemed to hang across it. "This is magnificent," I said to my mother. *Magnificent* was one of my words, at thirteen.

Five months later I stood in front of the same window staring through a similar rain. My mother had just walked into the family room and said, "Lee's been killed in an accident." Everyone called my father Lee although his name was Leland.

There was no lightning this time, only a steady downpour into which I had run to stop my mother's car. She was going shopping with my Aunt Doodles. "There's a phone call for you," I said, water running down my glasses. "It's Uncle Royce."

Aunt Doodles was with me in the family room when my mother came in and said what she said. Doodles began to scream. My mother slapped her, saying, "Stop it, Doodles, this is important."

And then my mother sat on the couch and turned to stone. My brother, who was five, and my sister, who was nine, were both crying, and Aunt Doodles lay down on the floor to moan. My mother sat stonelike on the couch and I stood by the window, growing fast.

Evil was the word I kept thinking. This yard, this rain, this giant live oak with its branches brushing the ground—it all looks harmless, but it's evil. I tried to absorb this new knowledge. I didn't care what else happened to me for the rest of my life, as long as I was never this surprised again.

Eventually I went over and stooped down in front of my mother because I knew she could not raise her head. Her eyes were like little black rocks. "What do you want me to do," I said.

"Make coffee. Get Doodles a glass of bourbon. Help your sister. I'm glad the sofas aren't being delivered today."

My mother was still furnishing the house. My father would never get to see the Victorian sofas placed at opposite ends of the long living room, although he'd seen the floors burnished, the chandeliers hung, the burgundy velvet drapes with the gauzy "sheers" between them that let in light, but would have stopped anyone from seeing in, had anyone tried to look. "Did I have breakfast with Daddy this morning?" I asked, and my mother stared at me without answering.

"Did I have breakfast with Daddy this morning?" I said again.

"I don't remember. Yes. Probably."

I put on a pot of coffee and got a glass of bourbon and water for Doodles, who drank it and quieted down, and I sat for a long time holding my sister, Marie.

Everyone loved Marie, who was cuddly and tender. She cried now with easy grief. "Listen, Marie," I whispered, "did we have breakfast with Daddy this morning?"

She shook her head, coughing with her tears. "He . . . he was *gone.*"

"He was gone when we got up?"

She nodded against me.

I got my mother a cup of coffee, put Lincoln Logs in the middle of the floor for my brother, and kept my arm around my sister, who continued to cry while people began to arrive.

By nightfall the house was full of quiet people, most of whom brought food. There were cakes and pies and casseroles and a ham and fried chicken and even a turkey. I wondered how anyone had cooked a turkey so fast. Maybe they had already been cooking a turkey and just decided to bring it over.

My mother refused food for ten days. "I was hungry," she told me later, "but I couldn't swallow."

At first I missed my father so much that, in the afternoons, while I was reading the newspaper on the floor of the family room, I would think I heard him whistling as he came up the front steps, and I would run out onto the porch before I remembered he was dead. I seemed to feel him everywhere, but gradually I realized that I only had three important memories of him in the few months we both lived at Black-lock. Over and over I took out these three memories and examined them.

The first was of him on the back steps by the kitchen, skinning squirrels. He had gone hunting out in our woods behind the rice paddies and had killed ten squirrels with a .22 rifle. Eight of them were shot through the head. I watched him peel a few of them, the tough gray skin slough-ing off to expose tiny pink bodies. He said it was no challenge to hunt squirrels unless you hunted them with a rifle.

"Are we going to eat those?"

"Nope. Your Momma won't let us."

"So what will you do with them?"

"I'll give them to John Tillman."

Tillman was the old black man in the bleached overalls I'd seen outside the gates the day we arrived. He'd been the caretaker of Blacklock for the previous owner, and for us he would continue to take care of the cows, do some plowing for a vegetable garden, and shoot the small alligators that roamed the rice paddies. John's wife, Ruby, was the woman I'd seen smoking the corncob pipe. Ruby could carry large bundles on her head, while I couldn't even balance a book on mine. The hateful young man I'd seen was their son, Junior.

"Niggers would eat those?"

"Who have you ever heard say *niggers?"*

"Uncle Royce. Momma. You."

"Don't say it ever again." He added, with a grammar I'd never heard him use, "Squirrel is good eating. Your Momma don't want to know about that."

The second memory was of a day I was in the house alone. My father showed up in mid-afternoon, carrying a paper bag out of which he produced a pint of fresh-shucked oysters, a stick of butter, and a half gallon of milk. He sautéed the oysters in the butter until their edges curled, then added the oyster liquor and the milk, seasoning only with salt and pepper. "The best things are simple," he said.

I did not often talk to my father and could not think of

much to say. Maybe my silence made him uncomfortable, or seemed like an invitation. While I sat at the kitchen table watching him eat a bowl of the oyster stew—I was not about to eat anything with whole living creatures cooked in it—he told me about electrons. "Electricity is a flow of electrons," he said. He talked for a long time about electricity, but the first sentence is all I remember.

My third memory concerns the first time I tried to use tampons. I'd started menstruating the year before we moved to Blacklock. I kept wanting to wear tampons, but my mother said they would stretch me so much that, when I was grown, my husband would think I was not a virgin. I could use the tampons I'd bought if I insisted, but she would not help me. I took my new box of tampons into the bathroom with a flashlight and a hand mirror. After an hour of examining myself I still wasn't sure what to do. The only likely place I could find for the tampon looked too small. The diagram that came in the box was hard to understand. So, when my father came home that evening, I was sitting glumly in the family room, and under my Bermuda shorts I was wearing a pad and belt. My father went into the kitchen to say hello to my mother, and I could hear them laughing. Then my father returned to the family room. He rarely looked at me so intently, or with such kindness. I could tell from his eyes that he had been laughing. "I love you, Ellen," he said.

.   .   .

There was a guest house on Blacklock, a four-bedroom, two-story house at the edge of the paddies, where my Uncle Royce and Aunt Doodles and their three children lived. And out at the edge of the pasture was an abandoned house that had never been finished. No doors hung in the doorways, no windows hung in the window frames, and no stairs existed to get up to the doorway. Yet someone had intended something serious here: the large stone fireplace had been built by hand.

In the woods behind the abandoned house was a graveyard. "Probably for the slaves, from when the house was first built," my mother said. But several of the half-dozen graves were marked by small stones with their inscriptions worn off, and I was told by my 4-H counselor that slave graves would not have had stones.

The graveyard was pocked with sinkholes full of rich, crumbly soil. Marie and I climbed around in several of them one day, half-heartedly looking for jewelry or bones.

Our father had been buried in a modern cemetery, where little brass plaques set into the ground identified who was buried where. Each grave had a narrow brass vase bolted to its plaque, so the grounds, instead of looking smoothly green, were punctuated by these short brass stalks, as if some strange metallic crop had been harvested.

In the graves behind the abandoned house my sister and I found nothing. "Imagine, Marie," I said. Marie was thin and her blond hair was always hanging across her eyes. "These people are nothing but dirt. Not even a good skull around." I held up a clump of earth. "These were the eyeballs."

Marie was wearing a pair of jeans she'd cut holes in. In later years she would claim to have been one of the earliest hippies, but when she was ten, she called her outfits "hobo clothes." Hoboes, she said, were the best people.

I held up a twig. "Maybe these were somebody's teeth."

Marie began to cry.

They had embalmed our father and buried him in an air-tight metal casket. Our mother said his body would be preserved intact for at least ten years. I knew there was no light in his casket, but I imagined him lying inside the box in a pale yellow light, like a figure in a wax museum.

I thrust a clump of woody fibers toward my sister's face. "Look, Marie, this is somebody's hair."

She didn't run or turn away. She just kept looking at me and crying. I rubbed the clump of fibers on her face because it was the meanest thing I could think of to do. "I didn't kill him, Marie. God killed him."

Marie grabbed me around the waist and hid her face in my shirt.

"The one in Sunday School," I said. "The one with the long hair. That's who killed him."

Marie, still holding tight, ran against me. She was trying to knock me down.

I stumbled backwards and landed on my butt, with her on top of me. I could feel her frail shoulder blades, her skinny shoulders. "I'll take care of you, Marie," I said. "I always will."

To get to the main house, Marie and I had to walk back through the pasture. We were both scared of the cattle. "Come on, don't be afraid." I was trying to make up for my cruelty.

There were forty Black Angus in the pasture, and they thought any human figure was out there to feed them. Our uncle said what was most important about the cattle was not to run from them. They were harmless but they were big, and if you ran they would chase you because they wanted to eat.

I held Marie's hand and we walked slowly through the pasture while the cattle surrounded us, lowing. "These cattle are from hell, Marie. Don't you think they're from hell?"

"The twelve disciples were hoboes."

When we got to the fence in front of the main house she pulled her hand away and began to pet the cattle as if they were no more frightening than kittens. "I think Jesus was nice," she said.

The cattle had come with Blacklock, and they were one more source of confusion for us. Before my father was killed, my mother had thought having the cattle was fun. They were registered, and she joyfully named several new calves: Marie's Joy, Ellen's Joy. "Those are dumb names," I complained, but secretly I was thrilled to have one named after me.

My father wanted me to raise a calf, but of course he would not have time to help me, so one afternoon a crew-cut man from the 4-H Club came out to the farm. He went with my mother and me out into the pasture to look at Ellen's Joy.

All of the cattle looked basically alike, so I tried to memorize my calf's face while I petted her dutifully. She seemed to be doing fine in the pasture without my help.

As we walked back to the house and the man was explaining how the pen should be built, I looked behind us. One cow was climbing onto the back of another. "Mom," I shouted, "look!"

She glanced toward the two cows and ignored me.

"Mom, the cattle are fighting!"

She was still ignoring me.

"Mom!"

"I *see* it," she said, and went back to talking to the man with the crew cut.

After he had driven his pickup truck out the green gate hanging between the white stone pillars, my mother was mad at me. "You did that on purpose, to embarrass me."

"How did I embarrass you?"

"Those cattle were breeding. You knew that."

"You mean . . ."

"Yes, that's exactly what I meant."

Actually I knew very little about breeding. The year before, my mother had given me a book called *Life and Love for Teenagers,* which I found terribly exciting but not informative. There was a diagram of a penis that I liked, but my favorite parts were the narrative examples: *Doreen is sitting in Malcolm's lap and she can feel that he is getting excited. "I don't think we should do this, Malcolm. . . ."* How, exactly, did she know that Malcolm was getting excited? Thinking like this made my hands sweaty and my underwear damp.

I told my mother that I felt kind of leaky, but I didn't tell her why.

"Oh, my god," Aunt Doodles said. Momma had told her, right in front of me, that I had a vaginal discharge. "I knew something like this would happen. It's all this country air. There are too many bugs out here."

"What have bugs got to do with it?" I asked, horrified.

"I don't know," Doodles said, "but I don't like living on a plantation very much."

My mother was afraid I had an infection, so after a panicky discussion with my aunt, she decided that someone professional would have to examine me, even though I was so young.

I was taken to a gynecologist. Dr. Post was a tall, heavyset man with a few gray hairs combed across his bald spot. I thought he looked so stern because he was embarrassed. My mother and aunt were in the room, and they seemed embarrassed too. Before we'd gone to the doctor, my mother had warned me that the examination might hurt a little but that I should be brave. So when Dr. Post put a piece of cold metal inside me—I couldn't see much because of the sheet draped between my naked knees, but I could feel it—I said, "It's okay, it doesn't hurt." He still looked sternly embarrassed. "It feels good, really."

My mother was giving me her grimmest look.

"It does feel good," I said to her, but she didn't look any happier, so I raised my head and leaned up on my elbows and laughed gaily over the sheet, looking at each of them in turn. "It tickles, really. It feels good. No problem."

Afterwards my mother was furious. "You did that on purpose," she said, "to embarrass me."

"I was trying *not* to embarrass you."

She insisted I had done it on purpose, and I could hear anguish in her voice. For the first time I was old enough to understand that my mother had been hurt in her life in ways I was not going to know about.

Moving to the farm and my father's death were not the only sources of confusion the year I was thirteen. If we were going to live on a plantation the way my mother wanted, if we were going to have twin chandeliers and burnished pine floors and crushed white oyster shells in a circular driveway, we were nevertheless going to go to public country schools, as my father wanted.

I'd enjoyed a sense of normalcy in our old neighborhood, where in the evenings the fathers were all outside watering their lawns, and in the mornings the children rode their bikes to school in little flocks. In the suburbs each grade had been a rite of passage, and the difference between being in the sixth grade and the seventh was enormous.

At Plaxton Grammar School there were only two classrooms, one containing the first to third grade, the other the fourth through seventh. My sister and I were in the same room because Marie was in the fourth grade and I was in the seventh. There were only five people in my class, so it was going to be easy to be valedictorian. Royce, in the first grade, was in the other classroom.

My teacher was an elderly lady named Mrs. Veranda, who used to yell, "Listen at me now! Listen at me now!" She didn't make me do the lessons because at my other school I'd already finished the texts she was using. She just let me read. I remember *Quo Vadis?* and *The Robe.* "These people know how to write," she said.

Across the hall, my brother was learning to put little balls on his quotation marks. Printed quotation marks had little balls at the tops of their curves, and Miss Kooder made her students print them that way too. When Royce wrote his first short story—about a little boy named Roy who meets Jesus on the school bus and is the only one to recognize him—he was praised by Miss Kooder. A very deep child, she said. Royce's quotation marks around the clumsy block-lettered dialogue had the little balls on them. "Hi, Jesus." "Hello, Roy!"

Royce was so smart he was soon competing with the second and third graders.

My memories of Plaxton Grammar School after my father's death are nightmarish and almost all involve doctors. One day, as we got out of the car at school, Marie slammed her hand in the door. At the sight of the nail on her index finger hanging loose, she fainted. My mother drove us straight to the emergency room, still wearing her bathrobe. I held Marie, her finger wrapped tight in the sleeve of my green crewneck sweater. "God, I can't do this," my mother kept saying, but she didn't cry, and I didn't either.

Another day, my mother and my aunt roared into the school yard right across the grass to the front door. My mother was wearing a mink coat and dark glasses. She whipped off her glasses and announced our situation right in front of the classful of kids: Our well's pipe casing had cracked, and we had drainage water coming in through our taps. There was a dead calf in the irrigation pond and we had to go get typhoid shots *right now.*

We rode into town in Aunt Doodles' station wagon, Marie and Royce and my cousins and my mother and my aunt and me. I didn't tell them I had known something was wrong last night. The water in my bathtub was brown and had little twigs in it. I had thought Blacklock was so creepy that maybe this stuff was normal for country water. There were fibers like the ones I'd rubbed on Marie's face, so maybe the people from those graves, now that somebody had paid them some attention, wanted to have living people drink them or use them in baths.

We got the shots, which itched and burned, and in the afternoon I walked down to the irrigation pond. The pond was surrounded by mossy oaks that left it almost perpetually in shade, and the surface of the water was covered with green algae that had a magical glow. Floating on top of the algae was a calf. I didn't know if it was Ellen's Joy or Marie's Joy or one of the others, because I could no longer remember what Ellen's Joy had looked like. Anyway, it was impossible to see the face of the dead calf, and I didn't want to walk out into the pasture and try to distinguish my calf from all the rest. I thought the dead calf was probably Ellen's Joy, it must be Ellen's Joy, and that night I ran a fever, which my mother said was from the typhoid shot.

My mother had bought her mink coat grimly. "Why

shouldn't I," she told me a few months after Daddy was killed. "I can afford it, so why shouldn't I."

"Is it cold enough here for a mink coat?" I didn't even know anyone who wore an overcoat on cold winter days. I wore a suede jacket.

"I'll wear it."

She looked tough and glamorous in the mink, especially with the dark glasses.

One afternoon a photographer came to the big house to take a family portrait. We didn't have many pictures of Daddy because he hated having his picture taken. The best photograph we had of him was a Polaroid I'd taken Christmas morning with the new camera. Each print had to be coated by hand with a preservative. I did a good job on the composition—he was sitting in his undershirt and slacks in his armchair, and for once he was looking at the camera—but I didn't do a good job with the preservative, so there are brown spots beside his head.

My father's accountant, Rusty, was a short bald man with a pot belly. An amateur painter, he borrowed the Polaroid snapshot of my father and painted a portrait from it. I guess my father's funeral had made a more vivid impression on Rusty than the tiny image of the photograph, because in the portrait my father looks distinctly dead. His skin is pasty, his expression lifeless. In his gray hand he holds a rolled blueprint. "Because he was always looking at blueprints in his work," Rusty explained in a hoarse, emotional voice.

The walls of Rusty's office were covered with calendars

with pictures of naked women on them. There must have been thirty of these calendars, and when I was in his office I never knew where to look. My dad didn't like for me to go into Rusty's office, though of course I always wanted to. One day Rusty led me reverently over to a picture of a blond woman lying on red velvet. "Most of these pictures are jokes," he said, "but this one is Marilyn Monroe."

Soon after Rusty's portrait of my father, he painted a companion one of my mother. She posed in a pink off-the-shoulder formal, the tone of which contrasted sharply with her grim expression. She hung both portraits over the twin fireplaces in the living room, and several times a day she would go in there and study them. "I look like a bulldog in a tutu," she said every time.

The family picture the photographer made was, she said, mousy. Mother had told us not to smile, so we all looked glum, lined up on a piano bench and leaning toward each other for space reasons. Since Royce moved, his part of the picture was blurred. This painted photograph hung beside the piano in the living room, across from the double fireplace.

The piano was a massive grand made of rosewood. "We've got to fill this living room with something," my mother said the day it was delivered from the antique store, although none of us played the piano except my father, who played by ear and only on the black keys.

My father thought the piano was excessive, but he liked to sit at it and fool around, his burning cigarette laid on a bass key and forgotten. The key soon had a charred place, a brown hole in the cream ivory.

After he died, I didn't want us to have the key fixed, and my mother said okay.

My sister began taking piano lessons. "When do I get to learn the black keys?" she asked the teacher.

If my mother was brave and glamorous during the day, she was scared at night. "There's not another white family for two miles, except for Royce."

She had the entire two acres of lawn around the house lit with floodlights, and we burned these lights all night. Sometimes I would get up in the middle of the night and look out my window at the blazing yard.

Mother had an intercom set up between Uncle Royce's house and her bedroom, and she slept with a loaded .22 pistol under her pillow.

One afternoon Uncle Royce came over to the house and took me out onto the front porch to teach me to fire the pistol. "You're the oldest," he said, "and you should know."

Uncle Royce was huge and taciturn, and I was unreasonably afraid of him, especially of his cigars.

He placed a brick against the base of the enormous oak tree whose branches brushed the ground, and we sat on the porch and fired at it. *Don't aim,* I thought of my father saying about marbles. *Think your way through the target.*

"You're a natural," Uncle Royce said, as the brick chipped and smoked. He took his cigar out of his mouth. "Don't ever take the safety off that pistol unless you mean to fire it, and don't fire it at anybody unless you mean to kill him."

"Is it really dangerous out here, Uncle Royce?"

"These are poor people around here," he said, "and they think we're not."

I was the valedictorian at Plaxton Grammar School and went on to Plaxton High, but my mother said she'd had enough of little balls on quotation marks and *listen at me,* so my brother and sister started attending expensive private schools in Charleston. I refused the offer of private school because I intended to be self-made like my father. It was too bad I wasn't poor and could afford the books.

At Plaxton High I made up for affording the books by locking them into a locker at the beginning of the year and vowing to remove them as seldom as possible.

My little brother came home each afternoon and ran up the stairs to take off his blazer and tie and white shirt. He reemerged in jeans and a sweatshirt and raced outside to join John Tillman, the caretaker, who was teaching him to kill and skin snakes and alligators, to shrimp out the rice fields, to shoot ducks at sundown. I didn't see how he could spend so much time with John Tillman, who spoke Gullah with such a strong accent that I couldn't understand him, even if I asked him to repeat what he'd said.

Marie and I began to lose touch, because she got busy being rich. The girls' school she went to was full of Charleston aristocrats, and soon all Marie cared about was clothes and manners. She couldn't have been more than eleven when she first criticized our mother's taste. The upstairs bathrooms, Marie said, were gauche. I didn't know this word yet, but I pretended to. The twin bathrooms had been painted pale pink and pale blue and they had matching square tubs, which I thought was rather thrilling. Marie said it would have been much better to leave the old tub, with its claw feet. She said this with considerable authority, wearing her little cotton shirt with its round collar, her A-line skirt, her loafers called Bass Weejuns.

I spent the beginning of high school getting ready for war with Russia, and learning to be a beauty queen.

Our father had bought the plantation not simply because he wanted to be in the country and hunt squirrels, but because Blacklock had water around nearly half of it: The river curved, the rice paddies were not easy to cross without being seen, and the main house was on a little rise. Blacklock, my father said, was defensible. He would have built a bomb shelter, had there been time.

I read a book on European communism called *The God That Failed* and a book on American communism called *Masters of Deceit*, by J. Edgar Hoover. The communists were everywhere, I realized. They could be anybody.

I lay awake at night and thought about the Red Threat. Probably nobody in my own family was a communist, and probably nobody in South Carolina was a communist. We didn't even have Republicans yet. We had some Jews and there were Greeks and of course there were the colored people, but they weren't like us.

Colored people went to different schools and they had no morals. Plaxton High was twenty miles from our house because the white community out in the country was a minority. My mother said not to pay any attention to the Freedom Riders, they were just communist agitators and Yankees who couldn't mind their own business.

I tried not to watch the Freedom Rides on television, but they were on the national news a lot, and the national news reporters acted like the Freedom Riders weren't wrong. They seemed to think the Freedom Riders were heroes.

We had a maid named Barbara who was sixteen and pregnant. She was going to get married in a white dress, and by the wedding date she would be nearly due. "We jus' keeps lettin' out de dress," Barbara said. She showed no sign of shame.

In private I asked Barbara if she thought, well, if she thought it was wrong to get pregnant before she got married. She was ironing sheets in the family room, in front of the television. "Why?" she said.

Barbara was a color like rosewood. Her brown eyes were so dark the pupils were not visible. Her large lips fascinated me.

"Because, because of . . . Jesus?"

"I loves Jesus."

My sister was practicing on the rosewood piano in the living room, and over the sounds of *Queen for a Day*, the program Barbara was watching on the television, I could hear a halting version of "Over the Rainbow."

"Barbara," I said in what I hoped was a winningly confidential tone, "do colored people want to go to school with us?"

"We has our own schools," she said, but she wouldn't look at me.

I tried to keep talking to her, but no matter what I said, she wouldn't look at me again.

The year I was thirteen, I grew six inches. There was a cruelty in this, as if my father's death had been a kind of fertilizer. *You look wonderful,* people began to say. *What's your secret?* By the time I was fourteen I was the height and weight I would be as an adult, and I had surprising breasts and smooth hips that I could feel moving when I walked. Everyone treated me differently, even my own mother. *Maybe the wrong one of us is in the fur coat,* she said.

If we didn't have war with Russia before I graduated from college, I was planning to be an FBI agent. In the meantime, my mother and I agreed that it would be wise to become a beauty queen. Beauty queens, my mother said, were graceful and well liked, and they had many travel opportunities. Each year we watched the Miss America pageant as seriously as we had watched the rereleases of *Gone With the Wind.*

So, in the eighth grade, after my hours at Plaxton High, I drove into Charleston and went to charm school, where I practiced walking with a book on my head, learned to wear makeup correctly and to speak in a pleasing voice. I practiced "judges' questions."

How do you feel about civil disobedience?

I feel that conscience is an important American characteristic, but without the law we have lawlessness, and lawlessness is always wrong.

I worried about my feet, which were very large. My fantasy of being a Cinderella beauty queen who would be swept off to Hollywood where I would fight the Red Threat was undermined by my feet. I would never wear glass slippers. My feet were so large they barely fit into women's shoes at all. *How do you feel about your feet?* Surely the judges wouldn't dare ask that.

The day of my first beauty contest, Ruby and John Tillman's cottage was robbed.

My mother had sent me straight into Charleston after school to have my face professionally made up. With my skin smoothed by foundation and powder, my color heightened by rouge, and my eyes artfully touched up, I thought I looked rather splendid. My hair had been set the day before, and I'd slept on a special pillow so it wouldn't get mussed.

I was lying in tepid water in my square pink tub when Marie knocked on the door. "Ruby's on the porch. She's crying."

Momma was still in town getting her own hair done, so I dried myself and pulled on some clothes as quickly as I could, then took my painted self out onto the porch.

Ruby was not on the porch but standing in the oyster-shell drive. She was wailing—a low, animal sound.

Ruby could carry large bundles on her head without touching them with her hands. She could plow behind a mule. She wore kerchiefs on her head and long skirts and men's work boots. She smoked a pipe. Two of her teeth were capped with gold. She looked like the black mammy in *Gone With the Wind,* but Ruby's Gullah accent was so extreme, like her husband John's, that she was barely understandable. "Ah beeen raab," she kept saying. "Ahhh, missy, I been raab."

I wished my mother were home, or Uncle Royce. Aunt Doodles might be over at her house, but in an emergency she was worse than useless. "Do you want me to call the police?"

"Ah, missy. Wha some un wan raab fo? It aina right. Ah, missy, ah, ah, ahhhh . . ."

I felt ridiculous in my beauty-contest makeup, my meticulously set hair. "I'll go get my gun."

Carrying my mother's pistol as if I were in a Western, I followed Ruby down the hill. My brother and sister stayed on the front porch, watching. I wouldn't let them come along. "If I'm not back in ten minutes," I yelled to Marie, "call the sheriff!"

"How do you call the sheriff?"

"I don't know! Ask the telephone operator!"

Ruby was snuffling now. I looked at the dark skin of her arm, graying with age as if it were dusty. "Did they take much?"

"Hatdag," she said. "Ho pown ubum."

I figured I'd know what she meant once I got to her house. I'd never been inside a black person's house before, and I was excited.

We stepped through the green gates hanging on the white pillars onto the dirt road overhung with live oaks and turned quickly into Ruby's dirt yard. "Ruby," I said, "you ought to plant some grass here," but she didn't seem to hear me.

The steps had rotted in places, and the porch was tilted forward. The front door had no lock. "You need a lock."

I pulled open the screen and pushed the door inward, holding the gun forward, but the silence of the house was utter, and I knew it was empty.

The living room contained our sofa from our other house; the stain on the armrest was from my father's hair cream. "Momma gave you this? I wondered what happened to it."

There was no other furniture except for a broken rocker. Pictures of food were tacked on the walls: a chocolate-frosted layer cake sliced open to reveal a yellow interior, a roast beef cooked rare, a pile of sugar cookies decorated with green and red sugar. "What a good idea," I said, not understanding yet.

There was a door off to the left, and straight ahead was the kitchen. Inside was a Formica table with rusted legs, two chairs with the stuffings sticking through, and an old refrigerator with the door held shut by a piece of wire.

The gun was making my hand sweat.

"Ruby, do you have running water?" There was no sink, but there must've been electricity because of the refrigerator.

Ruby unfastened the wire on the refrigerator and began to make that sound again. By the time she opened the door she was wailing. "Hat dag," she kept saying. "Pon ubum. Dey takum."

The refrigerator was empty. I peered into its white interior. "Hot dogs, Ruby? Are you saying hot dogs?"

She nodded.

"A pound of them?"

"Ho poun."

"A whole pound?"

She nodded again. "I habum fo de dinna. Some'un takum."

"That's all that was in here?" The sight of her large eyes weeping was beginning to terrify me. "That's all that was in the refrigerator?"

I backed out of the kitchen, pointing the gun at her. "Jesus," I had started to say. "Jesus, Jesus, Jesus."

Without asking permission I went into the bedroom. On the floor was a mattress covered with a handmade quilt. The window had no glass in it but was covered with a piece of milky plastic. The quilt on the bed was diamond patterned in green and red, like the sugar on the cookies in the picture in the living room.

Ruby came into the tiny bedroom behind me. "Jesus," she had started saying. "Jesus, Jesus, Jesus."

I won the beauty contest that night, but I was drunk.

One of the first things I'd learned at Plaxton High was to buy little bottles of spirits of ammonia in the drugstore and mix a few drops of the liquid, which was intended only for sniffing, with Coca-Cola, if I wanted to get high and relaxed.

My bright red formal had a hoop under it. Long white gloves with tiny pearl buttons reached above my elbows. A boned corset laced tight pushed my breasts up. The tiny bottle of spirits of ammonia fit easily into the silver mesh purse my mother lent me. My shoulders were bare, and I felt like Scarlett O'Hara.

All of the contestants were wearing *Gone With the Wind* dresses, but mine was the boldest color.

My mother and aunt were sitting in the second row, looking at me encouragingly as I crossed the stage carrying a little cardboard square with my number—12—on it. My mother was wearing her fur coat.

My mother and aunt had arrived home while I was giving Ruby the food. "What's happening here?" my mother had said.

Ruby was holding a brown paper grocery bag full of canned goods and a roast from the freezer, and she looked as frightened as if she'd been caught stealing.

I was acting guilty too. "Ruby was robbed. I'm giving her some food."

My mother walked over to Ruby and peered down into the bag. When Ruby tried to hand it to her, she said, "No, you keep it if Ellen gave it to you." But she reached inside and pulled out a can of corn. "I was going to serve this tonight."

"I left the pork chops in the fridge," I said from behind her. "I thought they were for supper."

When my mother turned toward me, I wished she weren't wearing dark glasses. She turned back to Ruby and put the can of corn back into the brown paper bag.

"Momma, should I have called the police?" I couldn't

bring myself to say what had been stolen, and, luckily, neither she nor my aunt asked.

"The sheriff wouldn't do anything. Shouldn't you be getting ready for tonight?"

As we went into the house I glanced down the oyster-shell road, watching Ruby's heavy figure move down it, carrying the groceries.

"Listen, Ellen," my mother said as soon as we were inside, "how do you know Ruby was really robbed? You've got to learn the facts of life. These people are like children. We'll have Ruby up here all the time now, looking for handouts. My god, your makeup has gotten messed up. Honey, have you been crying?"

The night I became Miss Plaxton High School I slept easily because of the spirits of ammonia, but I awoke to the sight of my mother leaning over me in my bed. In her shaking hand was the .22 pistol.

Momma's hair was wrapped in toilet paper held in place with long pins. Mine was too. We didn't want our hairdos to get messed up. My rhinestone tiara was on the night table, and I could see it out of the corner of my eye.

Momma was wearing a light blue nylon shortie nightgown. "Somebody just jumped through the dining-room window and landed on the silver tea service."

"Put the gun on the table, Mom," I whispered. I could see that she'd taken the safety off, and the trigger, I already knew, was quick.

She put the gun beside the tiara, clicking the safety back on. Tears formed in her eyes. "I heard something, I know I did."

"Did you call Uncle Royce on the intercom?"

She shook her head, and I understood at once that she knew she was just afraid.

I was halfway down the brightly lit stairs, a gun in my hand for the second time that day, when I realized what she had actually said. I stomped back up the stairs until I was eye level with her bony feet. "Are you crazy?"

The dining-room window was a window between two rooms. In her redecorating fervor, Momma had enclosed the back porch with a wall of glass, tiny panes that broke up the view of the rice paddies.

Her toes were moving nervously, like fingers. She was crying openly now.

"I'll go see. I'll go see."

Every light downstairs was burning, even the chandeliers in the living room. As I inched down the stairs, I wondered if she could be right. Maybe there was a killer downstairs. Or maybe she'd heard bombers and we had ten minutes to live. Maybe there was someone breathing in the living room. Maybe the intruder would step from behind a curtain. Maybe he would rise through the floor, like a figure in a horror movie. Anything could happen. I could be staring into the face of our killer and I would think, *This can't be happening, this can't be happening,* but it would be happening, and there would be an empty refrigerator and a rhinestone tiara, a glowing green pond with a dead calf in it, my father with ten skinned squirrels as pink as babies, then the bombs going off, the great flashes of light, and I would still be thinking, *This can't be happening.*

When I got to the base of the stairs I waited and listened. There was a tinkling sound, a faint bell I heard over the pounding of my heart. I reached around the doorway to the living room and turned off the lights without entering. Then I turned off the hall lights.

I made my way into the darkened living room, where the ghostly portraits of my parents glanced down at me. I leaned against the wall by the window, feeling like the star of a movie. Then I pulled back the red velvet curtains and the white sheers and looked boldly into the yard. The floodlights made it brighter than a shopping center.

Standing below me at the window was a skinny cow with a bell around its neck, munching our thick grass lazily.

I laughed out loud.

After I had mixed two bourbon and Cokes in the kitchen—it never occurred to my mother that I was drinking since I was so young—I put them on a tray with some peanuts and went back upstairs.

"Cow in the yard," I said as I put the tray on my mother's dresser. "So see, you did hear something." I handed her a drink. "This one is yours."

I got my tiara from my room and put it on my head right over the toilet paper, then got into my father's side of the bed. "What are you drinking?" she said.

"Coke."

She was smiling in spite of herself. "You look pretty silly."

"Not you. You look real natural."

As she drifted off to sleep, she said, "Ellen, I worked like hell for what I have. Nobody's going to take it away from me. Do you understand?"

"I understand better than I did," I said, thinking of the empty refrigerator, the pictures of food on the walls.

"Right and wrong are luxuries," she murmured, as if she could hear what I didn't say. "Your father and I grew up with nothing."

"Did you have food?"

"You have a tender heart," she said, "but you'll get over it."

I lay awake until almost dawn, drinking. I was a beauty queen, if you could count being Miss Plaxton High. I had a tender heart, but I would get over it. I had faced danger twice in one day with a gun in my hand, and I was just crying because I was drunk. I lay beside my mother in my rhinestone tiara feeling certain that I was the new head of the house.

Chapter 6

We moved out of Blacklock because of my stepfather.

"I don't understand why we're leaving," my brother Royce kept saying. "Those people aren't here anymore." He meant Dr. Post and his two daughters, who had moved back to their big house in the historic area downtown.

But the main house at Blacklock got boarded up, and soon we were unpacking our belongings in a house on a golf course in the suburbs of Charleston, where what we could see from the picture window was not fifty acres of ruined rice paddies but the flag flying on the fifteenth green. "B movie," I kept saying to Royce. "Our lives are just a B movie." But Royce, who was eight, was not interested in anything I said. He was interested in snakes and alligators and in the caretaker, John Tillman, whom he missed bitterly.

Our mother began dating Dr. Post when I was in the ninth grade. At first none of us liked him. He wanted Royce to say "yessir" to him. "Like I was at school," Royce said. And it bothered Marie that he was a gynecologist. "Extreme," she offered, a word of contempt in her circles.

Marie was mildly glad that Dr. Post belonged to the Yacht Club, that he owned an old house in Charleston, and that he dressed elegantly, but I had told her in some detail about his examination of me, dwelling on the part about the cold metal thing he put inside me. "Extreme," she said again.

Marie was blond and pale and I was so dark I looked Mediterranean, and Marie held still a lot while I was always restless, but people could tell we were sisters because we had the same slouch. Our necks were held forward, vulnerable as turtles, and we both liked to keep our arms folded across our chests, as if we were hiding something.

At first Mom said she had an appointment with her doctor for a routine checkup. Then we noticed she was going to the doctor a lot. Then she said she was having lunch with Dr. Post. "Lunch?" I said. "Lunch?"

My mother actually blushed, and I felt a coldness, a shiver that was like fury. "You call him Dr. Post and you're having lunch with him?"

"His name is Ernest," she said.

"Oh god," I said. "A gynecologist named Ernest Post, and my mother is going out with him. That's what it is, isn't it?"

"It's just lunch," she said. "And I call him Ernest."

"He's got no hair, Momma. Please don't do this."

"I'm a young woman, Ellen."

The first time Dr. Post came to dinner at Blacklock was in April, but the weather had already turned hot. Honeysuckle bloomed along the fences, making a smell like the perfume in a drugstore. Bees buzzed happily all over the yard, and bugs seemed to crawl along every available surface: the ground, the trees, the porches, the kitchen counters, our skin. "Did we have this many bugs in Charleston?"

Mother didn't bother to answer me but continued spraying Raid along the baseboards in the kitchen. She was wearing only her slip, and I could see perspiration gleaming along her shoulder blades.

"I found a snake in the laundry room," she said. "It was curled up right in front of the dryer."

"I'm never going in there again. I like my clothes dirty anyway."

"It was just a blacksnake, Ellen. You take a shower, and I'll take another one too. I don't want us smelling like bug spray." She was holding up a different can, an air freshener, as a cloud of mist formed in front of her. This smell seemed to be gardenia, but it was hard to tell because of the insecticide.

Dr. Post arrived wearing a blue seersucker suit, white shoes, and a white Panama hat. My mother came downstairs wearing an orange sundress, sandals, and lots of gold bracelets. She had told me to wear a dress but I said I had no intention of keeping my knees together in this weather, so along with Royce and Marie I was allowed to wear Bermuda shorts.

In the Victorian living room, Ruby awkwardly served us iced tea. She was wearing clothes like Aunt Jemima on the pancake-syrup bottle: a big flowered skirt, an apron, and a kerchief over her burly gray hair. As she offered around the tray of glasses, she didn't really look at anyone but me.

When Ruby left the room, Dr. Post remarked on the unusual smell in the house. Something perfumed but deadly, he said.

Mother smiled and began to explain how training Ruby seemed hopeless, but, really, what else did she have to work with out here? Barbara, our former maid, had stopped cleaning house for us after she'd had her baby. She'd had her baby on her wedding night, wasn't that amusing? Barbara hadn't known the first thing about serving food, and at least Ruby was trying to learn. Momma had asked her to wear a uniform but she said no, or managed to convey no while saying nothing, but that was typical, wasn't it?

Royce had put a plastic ice cube with a fly embedded in it in Dr. Post's drink and Ruby had gone along with his plan by making sure Dr. Post got the right glass, so I was thinking Ruby was pretty great and my mother was pretty awful. I hated seeing her nervous over a man who combed his three oil-coated hairs across the top of his head. It was fun to watch him sipping his drink. Either he didn't see the fly or he didn't choose to.

We had dinner in the dining room instead of the kitchen, and my mother had put the food in the good china serving dishes, which usually happened only on Sundays when my aunt and uncle and their children came over, and the table was set with the sterling silver, which happened only on

Christmas and Thanksgiving, and Ruby brought in the bowls of food, which had never happened.

Dr. Post's voice was sonorous and reassuring. "Please call me Ernest," he said to me.

"I can't," I said. "You know why."

During dinner our mother hardly ate. "She has the appetite of a bird," Dr. Post said.

"A condor," I said. This was not an original joke on my part, and Royce and Marie laughed too hard. Mom flashed a brief smile that could have been friendly in different circumstances.

Dr. Post grinned toothily and asked me what I intended to do about college. I felt certain he had rehearsed his questions.

I said I was going to Georgia Tech to study engineering and take over my father's business. I said I believed in my father's business and that it might seem to an outsider that he had just been a fancy plumber, though, of course, gynecologists could be viewed the same way, but actually the industrial-piping business required a great deal of technical knowledge, and anyway the authority of an engineering degree might help me overcome the workmen's natural reluctance to take orders from a woman.

"I had no idea you wanted to go to Georgia Tech," my mother said. "That's a wonderful idea."

"It is?"

"Ellen is such a tomboy," my mother said to Dr. Post. "I don't have to worry about her with boys. She'd probably just say, if a boy got fresh with her, 'Would you like to box awhile?' "

"I would?"

"She'd punch 'em out," Marie said.

"What is all this?" I stared up at the window that led to the enclosed back porch, the window through which the intruder was supposed to have jumped the night my mother got scared.

"Have you thought about medical school?" Dr. Post said. "Medicine is an exciting arena for an ambitious young woman."

"No," I lied.

"We have a very good medical school right here in Charleston. I'd be pleased to show you around sometime, if you're interested."

I glanced across the table at Marie, who was mouthing some word at me, and then at my mother, who said, "That's a wonderful opportunity for you, Ellen. I hope you'll take advantage of it."

I thought about making my fit noises. Sometimes at dinner I would feign epilepsy or insulin shock. My mother disapproved so strongly that she would send me away from the table. But sometimes she'd start laughing in spite of herself, and I'd feel close to her, because of our collusion in doing something wicked.

I glanced at Marie again, who was still mouthing something at me. It seemed an unsuitable time for a fit but I reasoned that I was only in the ninth grade and that my father had only been dead two years, and here was my mother dating somebody, so I picked up a piece of steak, tossed it into the air, and caught it in my mouth.

"Ellen!" my mother said.

"Sorry. Couldn't help it."

I looked at Marie again and realized she was saying the word *vagina,* so I threw the next bite of steak right across the table, where it splashed in her squash.

"Yaaay," Royce said. He threw a green bean at me.

Marie was holding her fork straight up by the handle and trying to use it like a catapult to launch a green bean, probably some maneuver she'd seen on TV. I only saw the fork poised for one second, and then everything seemed to be in slow motion as it left her hand with the bean. Then the fork was poised against my forehead, the tines stuck in my hairline. If Marie had practiced this move for years, she couldn't have repeated it.

The fork clattered to the floor. "You're going to marry our mother," I said to Dr. Post. "We can already tell."

Dinner was interrupted briefly while Dr. Post and I went into the bathroom together and he examined the fork punctures in my scalp. "We'll wash these with soap and water, just as a precaution, but they're hardly bleeding." I could smell him, standing close like that while he sponged off my forehead. He was wearing Old Spice. He seemed much more relaxed than when I had visited his office. "I think you're more comfortable with this end of me." He laughed out loud. I was starting to think Dr. Post might not be so bad.

. . .

117

The second time Dr. Post came to Blacklock, he brought his daughters, Glynnese and Hope, with him. We took a long walk through the pasture, out into the rice paddies, to the broken dam.

Hope, who was my age, went to the same private school Marie attended. She had a square face and eyes as large as Bambi's. She asked me real questions, like, *What do you think of our parents getting married?* And she told me, though I hadn't asked her, that her mother had died dreadfully. That was the word she used. Dreadfully.

Hope was wearing jeans and cowboy boots, but she walked gingerly, as if the grass itself was dangerous.

"I think it's great they're getting married," I said.

When she looked me in the eyes to see if I was telling the truth, I looked away. "That's my calf," I said, pointing to a cow at the edge of a group of them beginning to follow us. "That's Ellen's Joy. I was going to raise her for 4-H but it didn't work out." The cow looked the same to me as all the others.

"How can you tell that one's yours?"

"I know her face."

"Your cow's dead," Marie said.

"Shut up," I said. "What do you know?"

Glynnese clung to her father's hand and stared at my mother. She was only seven years old, a few years younger than Royce, who had refused to join us on the walk.

Hope told me Glynnese still sucked her thumb and was failing the second grade. "She just can't cope. Our mother started dying when Glynn was four, and it took her two years to do it, and Glynn was always spending afternoons at the hospital, and there was nobody to put her to bed at night except me."

Marie had been glancing over at me, to see what it was permissible to say, but this information was too much for her. "What did she die of?"

"Cancer, of course," Hope said.

"Of course," I said.

"Of course," Marie said.

"Why wasn't your father putting her to bed at night?" I asked.

"He was, when he was home, but he was at the hospital a lot, and he had to work, too."

We arrived at the dam, which was out near the graveyard. Before we moved to Blacklock I had thought, from seeing dams on television, that they must all be concrete and hold back enormous bodies of water. Our dam was a high dirt levee packed over rocks. It was supposed to protect the rice paddies from the Plaxton River, which was salty because we were only a mile or so from the ocean. My mother had just had the dam rebuilt, to try to reclaim the paddies. It would take at least fifty years, the 4-H man had said, before the salt would be gone from the dirt and the land could be planted. "What crops are we going to plant?" I'd asked my mother. "I mean, why are we rebuilding the dam? The rice paddies are kind of beautiful." She hadn't answered me. I know now that she had been trying to fashion Blacklock into a fantasy, but at the time I was genuinely puzzled. She was building stables, and none of us knew how to ride.

We stood on the packed black dirt of the dam and looked out over the long marshes the river ran through. The marsh grass rippled with every trace of breeze. "The original dam was built in 1748," Dr. Post said. "The early settlers tried to farm rice in South Carolina. Rice was not a viable crop here, and the economy soon prospered on indigo. The original house at Blacklock was built by John Salton, who was a friend of George Washington's, and George Washington probably slept at Blacklock more than once. Of course, the original house was not like the house is now."

"Why is he giving us a lecture?" I whispered to my mother loud enough for him to hear.

"He had the place researched," she said.

"The dam was rebuilt in the early 1930s," Dr. Post continued, as if he hadn't heard me. "Fifty acres of rich truck-farming land was worth the small investment of the dam. Unfortunately, in the hurricane of 1938 the dam was destroyed, as was, I'm sure you know, a great deal of the East Coast."

"Dr. Post," I said, "do you know how to shoot squirrels? Are you a hunter?"

"I've never cared for hunting," he said. "I do like sailing."

"It figures," I said.

On the way back across the pasture I offered Hope my own theory about the history of Blacklock. "Blacklock is cursed," I said. "See that little house over there? That house was abandoned before it was finished. There's a beautiful stone fireplace in there somebody built by hand. And there's a graveyard behind it, and we don't know who's buried in it. Something's wrong here, Hope. You can guess and guess and guess, but nobody's going to know what happened at Blacklock."

Hope smiled as if she liked me. "My dad said you were melodramatic."

"You can call it what you want, but nobody's ever going to know what happened at Blacklock."

The man who was driving the car in which my father was killed was named Skip. He was my father's chief foreman. The day of the wreck they were arguing about unions.

Skip wanted the company to go union; my father thought unions were communist inspired. He said he could do better for his employees on his own.

They were driving south of Charleston, almost to Savannah, to inspect a job. Skip said my father's attitude as a boss was not in question because he had always been fair, even generous. It was about being a working man or not. My father said he *was* a working man. Skip said you can't own the company and be a working man.

It was raining, and the windows were fogged. Maybe my father was thinking about how long they had been together. Skip was nineteen and my father twenty-five when they met. They were both plumbers, and my father told Skip to stick with him.

Skip stopped for a stop sign. My father was trying to look through the breath-fogged window when a car hit them from behind.

Skip's head slammed back, then forward, hitting the steering wheel. My father's head slammed back, then forward, hitting the dashboard. Skip cut his forehead, an injury that would give him a black eye. My father broke his neck.

Skip pulled him out of the car and put his ear to my father's chest. He was sure my father's heart was still beating, but the ambulance people said it was not.

Skip came out to Blacklock the afternoon of the wreck with several other workmen. They clumped through the big house in their heavy muddy boots and stood under the blinding chandeliers. They left tracks on the burnished wood floor. Skip's eye was swollen shut and he was sobbing. I had never seen a grown man sobbing. "I'm so sorry, Miss Irene," he kept saying. "I'm so sorry."

"Of course, Skip."

Skip stumbled past her into the downstairs bathroom, and we could hear him throwing up. "Get him out of here," she said to the other men. "Now." When they looked frightened she said, "He's in shock. I don't want him scaring the children."

Once my father was laid out, Skip refused to leave the funeral parlor. The casket was open, and my father looked very dead in it. His skin was a gray-green color I had never seen, except in crayons. Unlike Skip, my father was not marked by the accident. I thought that he should at least have a visible wound.

Skip spent the night sitting alone with my father's body. The funeral director said he would have to leave, but Skip didn't listen.

In the morning, before the services, I sat with Skip and held his hand. He looked strange wearing a suit and bow tie, especially with his eye bruised and swollen. "Daddy wouldn't want you to be acting like this."

"I'm saying goodbye." Still holding my hand, he rose unsteadily and walked me over to the casket. "Did you touch him?"

I shook my head.

"You should touch him," Skip said.

I reached gingerly into the casket, past the pleated satin lining, and touched my father's right hand, which was folded across his left. His skin felt like cookie dough.

Skip said, "Goodbye, Lee," and leaned over and kissed my father on the mouth.

Skip didn't think anyone should marry my mother, certainly not an aristocratic gynecologist who crossed his legs like a sissy. Skip said maybe my dad had bought a plantation, but he was still a regular guy who could shoot a squirrel through the head with a .22 rifle. He said my dad had just wanted a plantation to please my mom and because it was defensible from the communists, but this guy Post was the kind of man who thought he was better than the rest of us, and who wouldn't be interested in my mom if it weren't for her money.

When Glynn climbed the oak in front of the house and said that if anyone tried to come get her she would jump, it was Skip who went up there and got her down. "You'll have to land on me, honey, and knock us both out of here, but I'm probably big enough to catch you, so you might as well give up." But this happened almost a year later. At the wedding, Skip was fine.

The ceremony was held at an Episcopal church downtown, in a side chapel, with only the family and a few friends present.

The priest was a slight, red-haired man with a voice like a TV anchorman. His wife had huge breasts. I thought that was odd and tried to imagine the priest doing something with these breasts, but I wasn't sure what. Babies suckled, and teenage boys fondled, but what did priests do? My mother's breasts were so small I doubted Dr. Post would be interested in them, and I felt certain he would not be interested in her genitally. After all, he had examined her and many other women in stirrups. For him, it had to be all business.

I felt sick listening to my mother promise to love, honor, et cetera, and I was queasy too from the spirits of ammonia and Coke I'd drunk in my room just before we left for the church. Belching, I looked around the pews.

Hope was looking at me, and her large eyes seemed to be saying something. Had she noticed Mrs. Spratt's breasts? Everyone seemed comfortable and calm, even Skip, who had on his funeral suit and bow tie. His wife was wearing a champagne silk dress over her bulky figure. She held Skip's hand. I felt a ripple of envy and tried to pick up Marie's hand, but Marie reacted as if she'd been nipped by a dog. "Okay," I whispered, "okay."

The reception was held at Blacklock, in the living room, under the chandeliers. My parents' portraits had been taken down, because Dr. Post wanted it so, and they had been replaced by two elegantly framed watercolors of Charleston landscapes. Dr. Post had ruled out any appearance by Ruby in her Aunt Jemima outfit, so caterers were serving rare roast beef from a white-cloth-covered table, and slim black men in uniforms were serving canapés and champagne from silver trays.

I drank two glasses of champagne and went to talk to the priest.

"If you have two husbands," I asked him, "which one do you get reunited with in heaven?"

"I don't know," he said seriously. "There are many, many things I don't know."

"Are you going to let colored people into your church?"

"Of course. If they want to come."

"You're kidding."

His mild expression—it was hard to imagine his face looking anything but mild—was a contrast to his rich, powerful voice. I had never heard a Southerner express support of integrating the churches. "Are you a Southerner?"

"I'm from Georgia," he said. "God lives in some parts of Georgia."

"You're being ironic, aren't you? I'm trying to learn about irony. I think I might need it."

He had a funny little smile that I liked, so I said, "This is all pretty ghastly, don't you think?"

"Your mother remarrying?"

"You got that one correct. Do I have to call you Father?"

"Not if you're uncomfortable."

"Did you go to college in the North?"

"Yes, I did. Dr. Post is a fine man, Ellen. He's suffered a lot, and so have his daughters."

A waiter offered us glasses of champagne. Father Spratt declined but I took one and downed it in a swallow. "To irony," I said. "Where'd you go to school?"

"Harvard. Irony, you will find, Ellen, has its limitations."

I was beginning to feel drunk. "Did you know that there are people without enough to eat living right outside these gates?"

He didn't say anything for a few seconds. "So you see the limitations."

"Is your wife a patient of Dr. Post's?"

He laughed out loud. His teeth were as unremarkable as his physique. "Come and see me at the church," he said in that TV anchorman's voice. "We'll talk."

Marie and I liked to say the word *vagina* to each other in unacceptable situations. It was a code comment we thought was hilarious, so when Marie walked up to me and Father Spratt, I took into account that he was a priest and said, "The big *V*, Marie."

Marie was wearing her demure clothes and that matching look she had mastered since going to private school. "How are you, Father Spratt? I thought the service was very nice. You have such a wonderful voice."

"Marie is a hobo in her heart," I said.

"Thank you," Father Spratt said to Marie.

126

"Marie believes that the twelve disciples were hoboes," I said.

"How interesting," Father Spratt said.

Marie gave me a smooth look and turned her shoulder slightly, dismissing me. I left her with Father Spratt and went outside onto the porch.

Skip was leaning against a post and staring out into the pasture. He was drinking bourbon out of a silver flask he said my dad had given him. He offered me some.

"I better not."

Skip put his arm around me. "Pretty bad," he said.

"Maybe not," I said.

We walked slowly back inside with Skip's arm still close around me, and I could feel the strength of his barrel-like body. In the living room Skip made a toast. He said everybody loved Miss Irene and wished her well. I made a toast and welcomed Dr. Post and his daughters to the Condor family. Everyone laughed. "Good luck, Doc," I said, "you're probably going to need it."

Upstairs in my bathroom I got out a bottle of white shoe polish. Marie was right that the pink of this bathroom was too pink, and it was silly to paint one bathroom pink and one blue. Maybe our mother was gauche. Maybe we were all gauche. Marie was reading Faulkner at her private school, and she said we were a lot like the Snopeses. We didn't read Faulkner at my school.

Before I left I stared at myself in the mirror over the sink. I looked wild, and older than I was.

Outside, under the huge oak, I wrote JUST MARRIED on

the driver's side of Dr. Post's car. In smaller letters, on the passenger side, I wrote JUST REMARRIED.

I was fifteen, and my restricted driver's license allowed me to drive only between six A.M. and six P.M. I had a new car, a two-tone green Ford Fairlane, more of my mother's confusion, like the mink coat.

When Dr. Post and my mother emerged from the house with Hope and Glynnese and Marie and my Aunt Doodles trailing behind throwing rice, my mother looked as if she felt pretty silly, but she also looked happy. Dr. Post fussed about the writing on his black Lincoln in a way that let me know he was pleased. I don't think he realized that what the passenger side said was different.

When they got into his car, I raced to my own. "Come on!" I shouted.

Soon we were speeding down the oyster-shell driveway after our parents. Hope was in the front seat and Marie and Royce were sitting behind us. When Dr. Post's car shot through the white posts onto the highway, mine shot through right behind it.

We began to race down the highway together like that. I could see Mother laughing. She was saying something to Ernest, then looking back at us. We were laughing too.

My speedometer hit seventy, the fastest I'd ever gone. Then it hit eighty. "Cool," Royce said. "Wow."

My speedometer hit ninety. My mother's grin was stuck on her face. She looked worried and sad. She kept saying something to Ernest.

The two cars roared down the highway, and then Dr. Post

slowed to sixty. My mother turned around so we could see only the back of her head. We followed them that way for almost ten miles. No one said much. Hope was so silent I wondered if she was breathing. Royce said he had to pee. At Plaxton Junction I pulled off the road onto the gravelly space in front of the general store, and we watched our parents ride out of sight.

Chapter 7

At first our families adjusted to living together fairly well. Glynnese, especially, seemed happy. She began to call our mother Mom, and she sat in Mom's lap sometimes at night, although she was large for that. "My new little girl," my mother would croon, hugging her. I wasn't jealous, and I don't think Marie was either.

Glynn began to do better in school. She stopped stuttering and wetting the bed and started to tell jokes. *What lies in the grass and goes ding-dong? A wounded Avon lady.* She even began to talk back to her father sometimes.

Dr. Post's complaint about my mother's children was that we were smart-mouthed. Royce, especially, was difficult for him.

While our parents were on their honeymoon Royce killed a rattlesnake and nailed the skin to a piece of board; he placed the snakeskin prominently beside the front door and said it was a wedding present. When they got home looking tanned and satisfied, Dr. Post said this really was an interesting present, but he thought it shouldn't be on the front porch, especially not right beside the front door. I hated my mother's looking tanned and satisfied, so I said the snake was beautiful, look at the diamond pattern, and it wouldn't smell so much when it dried out. My mother said Royce was proud of the snake, so why don't we let it be there for a few days? That may have been when the trouble between Dr. Post and Royce started.

I liked Hope. She wanted to stay up late and talk after everyone else was asleep, and she drank her coffee black, which impressed me. We talked about death and she read me poetry. I introduced her to jazz. During the first summer we sat together on the glassed-in back porch until three or four in the morning wearing our dark glasses and pajamas, reading Kahlil Gibran and listening to Ahmad Jamal.

Mother and Dr. Post remodeled the family room and adjoining bathroom and part of the porch into a master-bedroom suite downstairs. All the children lived upstairs. Hope shared a room with Glynn because that was the way Glynn wanted it. Royce and Marie and I continued to have our own rooms, but mine adjoined Hope and Glynn's. Sometimes at night I would hear Hope saying, *Don't call her Mother. She's not your mother. Your mother's dead, don't ever forget your mother,* and in the morning I would try to talk to Hope about it, and she would seem reasonable, "Yes, of course you're right, let Glynn have this, she's happier," but then I would hear her again, *Your mother's dead, don't ever forget your mother,* and Glynn would be crying.

Hope told me about their mother's death, the baldness

from the radiation, the wig she wore, the thinness—"She always wanted to be thin, but not that way"—the large bruises, and, near the end, the swelling. I liked hearing about all this, because there was something vague about my father's death; he was there and then he wasn't. In a way, I thought Hope was fortunate.

Dr. Post wanted us to eat dinner in the dining room every day, and he wanted dinner served, and he said Ruby couldn't dress like Aunt Jemima anymore, so she wore a white uniform that made her look like a nurse, and when Dr. Post rang a little glass bell, she brought in the dishes my mother had helped her prepare.

One night Royce got sent away from the table because Dr. Post thought he was being mocked. Dr. Post ate the food on his plate in order. He ate all of his meat, then all of his potatoes, then his peas. Royce asked him why he was doing that. Dr. Post said that was the way he had been raised. "Holy cattle," Royce said. Royce liked to take expressions and change them. "Thanks fifty dollars," he would say.

It is true that Royce was not entirely tame. He was a little like our cat Eleanor. We had moved to the farm with two cats, Eleanor and Dixie. Dixie adjusted to the new house, but Eleanor now lived in the woods and no longer washed herself. Sometimes she brought a field mouse to the front porch and left it there for us to see, but she'd run away if we called to her.

"Holy cattle," Royce said again, and I noticed he had eaten all of his meat. He was starting on his potatoes.

"Do you like it like that?" Dr. Post said.

Royce nodded.

"You should say yes," Dr. Post said. "In fact, you should say yessir."

"Okay," Royce said with his mouth full. He kept chewing and didn't say anything else.

There was an awkward silence. Royce looked around innocently and swallowed his food. "Yessir," he said and started on his peas. He stuffed three forkfuls into his mouth, distending his cheeks, and began chewing again.

"I will not be mocked," Dr. Post said to my mother. To Royce he said, "I want you to go to your room."

The second time Royce was sent away from the table we were having spaghetti. Dr. Post ate spaghetti by wrapping the strands around a fork while bracing it against a spoon. He said this was the correct way. When Royce tried it, he dropped his fork. We all laughed and Ruby brought him a clean one. He tried it again and dropped his fork again. "I will not be mocked," Dr. Post said. This time Royce got up from the table without waiting to be told. "Can I take my plate?" he said to our mother. He looked as if he might cry. She nodded yes.

The next night Royce was not at the dinner table. "Royce had homework," my mother said lightly. "He asked if he could eat in his room, so I had Ruby take him up a tray."

Soon Royce never ate dinner with us. "I think he should be made to eat with the family," Dr. Post said.

"He will when he's ready."

"These children are spoiled."

"He's a little boy, and this is a hard situation for him."

"This situation has difficult aspects for everyone, and nothing is served by indulging a child."

"I'm not too crazy about these meals either," I said. "I think we ought to eat in the family room and watch TV."

Marie said, "I wish we could have hot dogs with chili."

"Broiled bologna and mashed potatoes," I said.

My mother looked so stricken I stopped. "Patience," she said. "I think we should all have patience with each other."

Hope and I got a lot closer because of all the hickeys I got one night at the Magnolia Drive-In Theatre. I had never heard the word *hickey* until I got about fifty of them. Hope was sixteen, and she didn't date because boys didn't seem to ask her out. I was sixteen, and I didn't date because my mother wouldn't let me. "There's plenty of time for that later," she said. "I want you to enjoy your youth." I enjoyed my youth by hanging out at the Magnolia Drive-In Theatre with my friends.

There was a huge yellow magnolia painted on the back of the screen facing the highway; the fee to enter was two dollars a car. Carloads of girls and boys from my high school arrived separately, and after my friends Janine and Marla and I had shared one or two of the beers that Marla was good at stealing from her father, we'd get out and walk around, presumably to go to the cinderblock bungalow where the magic square of light began. We bought popcorn and soft drinks and hot dogs that were suspiciously awful, but really we were looking to see who else was walking around.

Whether the movie was *Auntie Mame* or *Thunder Road,* we'd almost always seen it already.

In this way I ran into Jimmie Puckett, who was six feet four and hunch-shouldered. His upper lip overhung his lower one, and he always sounded as if he had a cold. He had on his basketball jacket.

Jimmie had never said a word to me before. He had a girlfriend whose upper lip drooped the same way his did. Her name was Sam. She was usually wearing his basketball jacket.

"Hi, Ellen," he said.

"Where's Sam?"

"She went with her mother to Greenville for the weekend."

"Drag for you, huh?"

He smiled, or smirked. "Want to eat some popcorn with me? My treat."

Jimmie and I got into his car, and after some popcorn preliminaries he began to kiss me on the mouth. I was not a particularly experienced kisser, and it was hard to breathe. I tried to like it, and after a while I did. Periodically Jimmie would stop kissing my mouth and suck on my neck, which stung, and eventually I said, "Hey, that hurts." He didn't stop, but he did switch sides.

Just before the movie ended, I thanked him and went back to the concession stand to go to the bathroom. Really, I wanted to see how my mouth looked. Would it be puffy and pale, like Maddalena's in *La Dolce Vita?* Would my mother be able to tell I'd been kissing?

My lips were puffy and pale, but what was that thing stuck to my neck? I pulled my shirt collar aside. The right side of my neck had ten or fifteen reddish-purple marks. I pulled the shirt collar to the left. The side he'd started on had a large birthmark-like splotch the color of raw hamburger.

I kept turning my head, first to one side, then the other, trying to understand what had happened to me. The light in the bathroom was pale and yellowish, and the mirror was cracked. I felt as if I'd stepped into a horror movie. A girl walked into the bathroom behind me. "Oh my GOD," she said, "I've never seen so many HICKEYS!"

Actually there were forty-seven, although Hope and I weren't sure how to count the ones that had merged. We estimated, using a dime for size.

I cried all the way home in the car with Marla and Janine, slunk past my mom, who didn't seem very interested in me because she was watching TV with the earnest doctor, then went straight upstairs and asked Hope to come to my room. She was wearing a black judo outfit that her mother had bought her on a trip to Miami. Hope had some weird clothes, but she wore them only in her own room. In public she dressed not to be noticed. I closed my door behind us and started to cry as soon as I showed Hope my neck. She put her arms around me and began to shake and I thought she was crying out of sympathy, but then I realized she was laughing. Hope never laughed. Even though I was still crying, I began to laugh. "Listen," I said, "this is serious."

"I *know,*" she said.

Hope got me two of my mother's tranquilizers and helped

me concoct a plan. She said it would take at least four days before the hickeys went away, and that I could wear turtlenecks to school. It was very important that her father not see the hickeys because he might know what they were, but probably I could get my mother to believe anything.

The next morning I hunched around school in my black turtleneck, trying to look as if I didn't have a neck. When I got home in the afternoon, my mother was in the family room practicing the cha-cha by herself. She and Dr. Post were taking dancing lessons together, but Mom did a lot of extra practicing. "Hi, Mom!" I shouted and breezed past her upstairs, where I drank a little spirits of ammonia—by now I liked it fine with just water—and waited a few minutes, practicing my lines, before cha-chaing down the stairs. I cha-chaed into the family room and danced right up to my mother. "Oh, Mom," I said, "look at this weird rash on my neck." I pulled the turtleneck down on the most heavily marked side.

My mother stopped dancing. I could see her mind working. "You've got to go to a dermatologist," she finally said.

I kept cha-chaing. "No way. It's just a rash. Janine Harris had it all over her stomach and it went away in a few days."

"Okay," she said, starting to dance again, "but if it's not better in a few days, you're going to a doctor."

I thought I would always be close to Hope, because of the hickeys.

I could say our families broke up because we couldn't

agree about integrating the churches, or I could say our families broke up because of the pig roast where Skip got drunk,
or I could say it was because Dr. Post was mean to Royce,
or because Glynn began to do loud, hostile burps at the
dinner table, or because Hope cut up the clothes Mom
bought her and cut her wrist as well. I could say it was
because Mom was naive enough to believe me about the
hickeys, or because she didn't know I was drinking her bourbon, taking her tranquilizers, and spiking my Cokes with
spirits of ammonia, or I could say it was because we had to
have those ghastly family dinners with Ruby serving in that
white uniform like a nurse's, and one afternoon her son
Junior went crazy and started shooting our cattle. Or I could
say it was because I went to see Father Spratt about the
hickeys, and he put his hand on my breast.

But I think we broke up because of the house.

First we were in a hurricane.

It was Mom's theory that Blacklock was in a storm chan-
nel. There didn't seem to be any other explanation for all the
lightning. When we'd lived in Charleston, thunderstorms
were common in the summers, and the lightning was often
close. We would count the seconds between the flashes and
the noise. Anything under five seconds caused us to shut off
the lights and sit on the beds and wait. But at Blacklock there
was no time between the lightning and the thunder. In one
storm the pecan tree right beside the house was hit. In another the lightbulbs in my bedroom exploded. In another a
ball of fire came through the kitchen door and went out the
window. "I don't think this is normal," I kept saying to

my mother, and that's when she came up with her storm-channel theory.

"I think there's a kind of corridor the weather passes through. Remember the lightning storms when we lived in Charleston? Well, that lightning had to be hitting somewhere. Now we know where it was hitting." She tried to make it sound logical. "It's atmospheric."

Of course, Hurricane Gracie didn't just hit Blacklock; it hit Charleston and south of Charleston. The eye went across Edisto Island, thirty miles south of us. I was disappointed about the eye. I had wanted to feel the sudden stillness in the midst of a storm, then the massive wall of wind.

"You're just so melodramatic," Hope said while we were getting ready for the hurricane together. Our job was to tape the windows in the living room. We had moved the heavy burgundy velvet drapes aside and were standing like lumpy ghosts behind the white translucent sheers, stretching masking tape across the panes of glass.

"This stuff won't do any good," I said. "We'll be surrounded by water. Cut off from civilization. If we live, it'll take the rescuers days to reach us."

"I think the windows look cute this way," Hope said. "Your mother can leave the tape up to help keep people from looking in."

"You don't like my mom, do you, Hope?"

"I like her."

"She's kind of nice when you get to know her."

"I like her," Hope said.

When we finished the windows we went into the kitchen,

where my mother was counting out candles. She had finished filling the kerosene lamps. "Take two candles each to your room, girls, and put some in the other bedrooms too."

I tried to see my mother the way Hope saw her: a woman with money and smart-assed children who was trying too hard to get her stepdaughters to like her. A woman her father had fallen in love with. An object of hate.

Mom was wearing blue jeans and a man's white shirt with rolled-up sleeves. I kissed her on the cheek. "Tonight we drown," I said.

Royce, it turned out, nearly did.

After the wind came and the power was off and we were all creeping around the house in the yellow glow of the kerosene, when it was too dark to do much besides wait, Royce opened the front door, went out onto the porch, and got blown off.

It was impossible to see anything through the howling hole of the door, and Dr. Post wouldn't let any of us go out to try to get Royce back. The wind was making a tremendous noise, and water was blowing into the hallway.

My mother was shouting "Royce! Royce!" into the dark, and her face and shirt were soaked from the rain. "God damn it," Dr. Post said when Royce didn't come back. "God damn it," he said again. He told my mother to stay in the house and then, holding a large flashlight, he stepped through the large doorway and disappeared too.

He came back carrying Royce, and they were both as wet as swimming. Dr. Post was mad, and Royce was crying.

"You little fool," Dr. Post said. "Somebody's got to teach you something."

I think Royce was humiliated because he was crying, and because Dr. Post had helped him, or he wouldn't have said what he said. "You fat old creep," Royce said. "I hate you."

I think my mother slapped Royce because she wanted to stop Dr. Post from doing it, but Dr. Post got to Royce anyway and picked him up by his shoulders. Whatever it was he intended to do, he stopped in midair and put him down. "That is it," Dr. Post said. "That is really it."

Marie was crying out of fear, and so was Glynn, and so was I. "Well," I said, sniffing, "what about the hurricane?"

For a moment we all listened to the roaring of the wind. The house was shivering. "You kids should all go to bed," Mom said. "Royce, go change your clothes and go to bed."

"You bet I will," Royce said.

We all watched Royce disappear into the hallway and listened to him stomping up the stairs without even a candle to guide him. There were stains, black in the dim light of the room, where he'd been standing.

"You should get out of those wet clothes, too," my mother said to Dr. Post. He was still staring into the hallway where Royce had gone. "Honey, you should get out of those clothes."

"Will we be washed away?" I asked.

"Of course not," Mom said. "We're on a hill."

"What about Uncle Royce and Aunt Doodles and Scooter and Sally and Diggs?"

"We're all going to be fine," she said, and I could hear in her voice the stoniness of the day my father died.

"I'm going to walk up those stairs with a book on my head," I said, grabbing a volume of the *World Book* set beside the television. "Like Ruby. Like a beauty queen. I've changed my mind about being a doctor. I've changed my mind about being an engineer." I put the book on my head and stood the way I'd been taught in charm school. Then I moved my head carefully around and peered at them standing in the gold light of the kerosene lamps. Glynn had her face buried against my mother's hip, and my mother's hand rested on her shoulder. My mother's other arm was around Marie. Dr. Post looked lonely, and so did Hope. The book slid off my head. "I'm just not good at this," I said.

Later my mother came upstairs to tuck us in. Hope and Glynn and Marie and I were all piled together in Hope's bed. Royce was in his own room, in the dark, with his door shut.

Mom sat down on the edge of the bed. "Quite an adventure," she said brightly.

"Mom," I said, "what about Ruby and John Tillman? There are trees hanging over their shack."

"They're farther from the river than we are," she said, "and I'm sure they've lived through worse than a little hurricane."

"Do they have lamps and candles?" Marie asked.

"I hope so. What soft hearts my girls have." She put her hand on Glynn, and Hope turned her face away. "Are you all right, Hope?" my mother said.

"I'm all right."

"Try to sleep," Mom said. "Ernest talked to Uncle Royce on the intercom, and Royce picked up some information on his shortwave. We're surrounded by water, but it's low tide, and it won't get any worse."

"What about the cows?" Marie said.

"I don't know, honey. They'll go to the high ground, I guess."

"If they can," Marie said.

"If they can."

"Momma," I said, "is everything ruined?" She knew I didn't mean about the storm.

"I don't know," she said after a few seconds. "Probably not. It takes a lot to really ruin something."

In the morning the light was gray, and the wind had slowed enough so we could all go out safely. The rice paddies were flooded. Trees were down across the dirt road, so we couldn't leave, and branches littered the ground like huge dark cobwebs. The giant oak in front of the house had split at its center. It hadn't fallen, but there was a great raw V of exposed blond wood oozing sap. I climbed up into the tree and looked into the hole. The center of the tree was hollow, dark, rotten. I knew from General Science class that trees die inside first, from the heart.

One night not long after the hurricane, while the electricity was still off, Uncle Royce and Aunt Doodles came over after dinner and the grownups had drinks together, and an argument started.

I was also having a drink, a bourbon and Coke, but no one knew that except Hope, whom I had started calling Hopi, because she had begun wearing a turquoise-and-silver bracelet her mother had given her. Dr. Post didn't want Hopi wearing the bracelet all the time, so of course she did.

Hope wasn't drinking so she didn't argue. She did listen with her lips moving slightly, mouthing an Indian chant she had taught me that went something like *nitchi tai tai, enui, nitchi tai tai, enui.* "You're just hostile," I'd told her when she developed this habit. "No," she said, "I'm just calm."

Uncle Royce said the niggers wanting to go to our churches were ridiculous, and my mother said they didn't want to go to our churches anyway, they were just trying to be trouble for us, and Aunt Doodles said it was the outside agitators, Northerners, communists, and Uncle Royce said it was FDR's fault and the day would come when people would spit when they heard that bastard's name.

"What is FDR's name?" I said.

"Franklin Delano Roosevelt," Uncle Royce said as if he were spitting.

Dr. Post said it was a matter of principle, the churches were for anyone who wanted to enter them, and my mother said principle shminciple, and I said I agreed with Dr. Post and my mother said my dad would've been ashamed of me.

There was a strange silence, as if everyone knew my mom should not have said that. "Maybe he would have been wrong," I said.

So that is how, on the Sunday when everyone knew that small groups of black people were going to show up at white churches all over Charleston, Dr. Post and I ended up riding together to church in his black Lincoln that felt like a hearse. My mother was furious. Hopi wasn't with us because she had taken to saying things like "I no longer believe in the Christian god," and when Dr. Post would try to argue with her she would just say *nitchi tai tai*.

"I'm impressed with your sense of principle," Dr. Post said.

"Is that what it is?"

I was worried about Father Spratt, whom I hadn't seen since the hickeys. None of us usually went to church anyway, and I couldn't understand how I had gotten myself into this situation.

"I'm really glad you're so close to Hope," Dr. Post said. We were driving across the marshes, and the marsh grass was rippling like hair. "I wanted to ask you, do you think Hope is all right?"

"Yes," I said, lying.

"I want her to get close to your mother."

We were going past the Plaxton Country Store now, where I often got sent for staples: bread and milk and Coke. The nearest supermarket was ten miles away.

My bra felt too tight. My blue sheath dress was a bad choice. Why had I worn a dress with no sleeves? Bare arms were too close to bare breasts. Maybe Father Spratt would be so distracted he'd give the wrong sermon, talk about David and Bathsheba instead of Jesus. Maybe the choir would sing Elvis's "I Want You, I Need You, I Love You," instead of "Red and yellow, black and white, they are pre-

cious in his sight, Jesus loves the little children of the world."
I wondered if Jesus just loved the little children, and if the
adults were another matter.

"How well do you know Father Spratt?" I said.

I'd gone to see him in my turtleneck to ask about lust, and
we'd sat on the sofa in his little oak-paneled office that was
lined with books, and I could see old gravestones out the
window over his shoulder. Father Spratt told me about
David and Bathsheba and the Song of Solomon, and his rich
voice was like a drug. He said that desire was a gift from God
and the right use of desire was one of the tasks of being
human, and he said that I was a lovely young woman and
he was moved by my questioning, so I pulled down the cowl
of my shirt and showed him my neck. "It's all right, Ellen,"
he said and touched my neck lightly and I started to cry, and
he put his arms around me in his fatherly way. With my
head down I saw the stirring in his pants. "Jesus," I said.

"Jesus, in my view, is the key to everything," he said. I felt
a thrill that must have been the light of God because he
started talking about desire being the light of God as he put
his hand on my breast. The light turned dark and awful and
I stood up.

"What was Harvard like?" I said. "I wish I could go to
Harvard."

Father Spratt got flustered and said he was very sorry, he
shouldn't have done that, and we're all human and frail, and
I said maybe he'd just never seen so many hickeys, forty-
seven actually, although it was hard to know how to count
the large patch.

"I've known Bill Spratt for a number of years," Dr. Post said. "He's a fine man, and I admire his courage. There are ministers who are less principled."

"His wife has big breasts," I said.

Dr. Post glanced at me. "That's a strange remark, Ellen. I'm surprised at you."

"I just think it would be hard for your posture."

"It is, in fact. Some women have to have breast-reduction surgery. I have several patients who made that choice because of back problems." He seemed pleased. "I think you'll make a fine doctor."

"Good, because I don't think I want to be a beauty queen anymore."

I'm photogenic or else I have bad luck, because otherwise I wouldn't have ended up in a photograph on the front page of the newspaper standing by some very respectable-looking black people in their church clothes. "This is the absolute end," my mother said. "How can I show my face in public?"

"You?" I said. "I'm the one with the problem." We were getting some hate phone calls saying I was a nigger lover, and at school the principal had called me into his office to talk to me. He didn't want Miss Plaxton High, who represented the school, being in the paper this way, and had I really thought through what I was doing? Didn't I know that letting the colored people into the churches would let them into the schools, and Plaxton would be overrun with people who couldn't learn, who smelled bad, and who were descended from apes? Is that from the Bible, I asked, and he looked at me like I might be talking smart-assed, but I was thinking about Jesus and David and lust, and he said yes, it was from the Bible, that Cain killed his brother Abel and Abel went to the land of Nod and married a bear because there weren't any other people, and that's where the black race came from. The land of Nod is in the Bible? Like Wynken, Blynken, and Nod? Marrying bears? You're very bright, Ellen, he said, but you've got to live in reality, that's the problem with being too smart, people who are too smart end up poorly adjusted.

He didn't officially suspend me, but he asked me to stay home for a few days.

My mother was ashamed to face her friends from the country club and didn't play golf for a week, but she was okay with me, probably because Dr. Post said I was brave. She said everything would blow over just like any other storm, just like the hurricane, and she sang, *When you walk through a storm, hold your head up high, / And don't be afraid of the dark* and hugged me, saying next time she hoped I would show better sense.

Maybe it was the hurricane, or maybe it was the uneasy alliance between Dr. Post and me, but we had several months of relative peace. Hope still wore the turquoise-and-silver bracelet and mumbled *nitchi tai tai* a lot, but two or three Saturdays she and Glynn went shopping with my mother, who bought lots of new clothes for them. Royce started coming down to dinner and saying things none of us could understand because he was trying to learn to speak

Gullah like John Tillman and Ruby, and Dr. Post didn't get mad at him but explained that Gullah was a dialect that needed to be preserved. He even said he was proud of Royce. I began to sleep without drinking the spirits of ammonia, although once or twice I lay awake at night and thought about the snakes the workmen had found under the house when they'd walled in the foundation. I knew the house was just sleeping.

The day of the pig roast, Junior Tillman shot two of the cows.

I had gone shopping with Mom and Hopi. Hopi was acting pretty strange. Mom had kept us home from school as a special treat because, she confided to me, she was concerned about Hope. She thought the three of us being together might help.

In the department stores Hopi quoted Kahlil Gibran and whispered to herself. "Don't worry about it," I muttered to my mother, "it's religious." I was getting nervous about her myself. In the dressing room, trying on jeans, I'd seen where she'd tattooed herself. On one thigh she'd written DEATH in small letters upside down, and on the other thigh she'd written HEAVEN right side up. That was the hard one, she said, she'd had to do it in front of a mirror. She'd dipped a heated pin in fountain-pen ink.

"I don't think this is so great, Hopi. That shit will never come off. What about when you wear a bathing suit?"

"I've changed my name to Serena," Hope said. "Please call me Serena from now on. I never go anywhere in a bathing suit."

But the clothes she wanted seemed normal enough, and the way she thanked my mother seemed sincere, and in the car, riding back out to Blacklock, although she was humming to herself, it wasn't that *nitchi tai tai* stuff, it was "Poinciana" by Ahmad Jamal. I decided not to tell about the tattoos. What if Hope told about the hickeys?

When we got home, two police cars were in the yard, their red lights flashing. Skip and Uncle Royce stood beside a cop whose wide hips were draped with a black holster and a truncheon. A shotgun leaned against one of the cars. Mom was scared something had happened to little Royce, but he was still in school.

Skip and Uncle Royce were drinking beers, and a cigar hung out of Uncle Royce's mouth.

Probably Dr. Post shouldn't have asked Skip to be the one to cook the pig, because didn't he know Skip hated him? But to cook a pig you have to dig a pit and burn hickory and oak to make coals, and you have to stack cement blocks and put a big wire grate over it and lay the split pig across, and for fifteen or twenty hours you have to tend the pig, basting it and keeping the coals just right. Skip knew how to do these things best.

Dr. Post thought he and Mom needed a party. He wanted his friends from the Charleston Sailing Club and the American Medical Association to see his plantation and meet his wife.

I don't know why Junior Tillman shot the cows. Maybe he could smell the pig roasting. Maybe he was tired of seeing his mother come home in that nurse's uniform. Maybe he was tired of seeing his father hanging around the fields with Royce. Maybe he was just drunk.

Skip and Uncle Royce were drunk. They'd been drinking since midnight, while they tended the pig. The pig pit was in the side yard, where there was a wide lawn with the two big pecan trees, so they didn't see Junior come onto the place, they just heard the shooting. When they got out to the pasture with Uncle Royce's shotgun, there were two cows on the ground, and Junior was sitting quietly, leaning against one of them. Uncle Royce would not have shot Junior if he hadn't reached for his gun again. Junior was lucky to be hit only in the arm, even if it was his elbow. Skip said he should have killed the bastard, but Skip just talked like that. Uncle Royce had loved the cows, he fed them every day, and he was upset over shooting Junior too. He said the meat was ruined because the cows needed to be bled sooner, and they were too old anyway. A truck from Mack's Meats would be out soon to pick up the bodies for disposal.

Mom said Junior was a bad one, she'd always known that, he had trouble written all over him. What a shame for Ruby and John, who were good as gold. The cop had a sheepish look because he was on a plantation with rich folks. He said it was the trouble with the churches and the outside agitators, and I turned my face aside because I was afraid he might recognize me from the paper. I said I was going down the hill to see Ruby.

Momma said no you're not, you stay away from down there, and I said if I'm an outside agitator why don't you shoot me too, and Skip walked down the hill with me and put his arm around me and said he loved me like a father, and none of this would have happened if Momma hadn't married Dr. Post. I hadn't seen Skip since the wedding and I sure didn't want to see him right now, so I said you've got to let me do this, Skip, I'm sixteen years old. I could feel him watching me walk through the gates.

I turned onto the bare dirt patch in front of Ruby's shack. Call me if you need me, Skip yelled, and I was suddenly afraid.

Ruby was lying on our old sofa with her kerchiefed head on the spot that was oil-stained from my father's naps. I could see her through the screen door. When I asked if I could come in, she didn't respond.

I opened the door and entered, glancing around at the pictures of food. The wedding-cake picture was new. Ruby sat up. "John go witum," she said, and then she started to make that low sound like music. I sat beside her on the sofa while she rocked back and forth. Soon I was rocking back and forth too.

"Ruby, was it because of the food?"

I'd been giving Ruby food out of the freezer ever since the day she'd been robbed, telling her it was a present from Mom, but I hadn't gotten up the nerve to tell Mom I was doing it. There was so much food in our house I didn't think it would be missed. "Did Mom find out about the food?" But all Ruby did was make that wailing sound. I tried to hold her dusty hand. "Gwan home," she said.

"You want me to go home?"

"Gwan home. Gwan home. Gwan home," she said, and so, quietly, I did.

It was a mistake for Momma and Dr. Post to go through with the party, but they said they'd already lost two cows and they didn't want to waste the pig, which was perfectly cooked, and there were too many people to call to cancel now.

I felt so weird I drank half a bottle of spirits of ammonia with no chaser, threw up, then went to sleep.

When I awoke, it was dark. I was disoriented and my head hurt, so I went to the window to look. The brightly lit yard was full of people in casually elegant clothes. There didn't seem to be anybody else upstairs, so I drank more of the spirits of ammonia, mixing it carefully with water. I don't remember much of anything for a while, and what I do remember is in pieces.

Skip was pushing Dr. Post and Uncle Royce was trying to stop him.

Hope had cut her wrist in the pink bathroom, a bracelet, she said. She'd cut it all the way around but not deep, part of a ceremony. But the blood clashes with this dreadful pink color your mother actually likes, she said, and she was smiling.

My tiara was lying twisted on the floor of my bedroom, its combs pulled off.

My mother was holding the clothes she'd bought Hope, which had been cut into strips, and saying to Dr. Post that Hope needed to be in a mental hospital.

Skip was knocking Dr. Post down, and Dr. Post got back up and hit Skip.

"I hate niggers," I said to my mother. "Is that what you want?"

To one of the guests, a frightened blond woman getting into a white Mercedes, I said, "Don't you want some more meat? We have a lot of meat around here."

Glynn had climbed far up into the heart-split oak in front of the house, and she said if anybody came up there to get her she would jump, but Skip, whose lip was bleeding, said, "You'll have to land on me, honey, and knock us both out of here, but I'm probably big enough to catch you, so you might as well give up." Then he climbed into the black heart of the tree and carried her down.

Dr. Post was putting Hope into his Lincoln. Hope's wrist was wrapped in a towel because it needed stitches. "It doesn't hurt," Hope kept saying.

I fixed myself a big plate of barbecue and sat on the front steps eating it as fast as I could. The last thing I heard Dr. Post say to my mother, as he got into his car, was "Honey, I just can't live in another man's house."

Chapter 8

The main house at Blacklock was boarded up for fourteen years. Uncle Royce and his family stayed on the place but didn't want to live in the main house. Too much trouble to move, Uncle Royce muttered, his unlit cigar in his mouth. Behind the plywood that was nailed over the big front doors, my mother's burgundy velvet curtains accumulated dust, the chandeliers stayed unlit, and my sister's grand piano turned gray from lack of wax. There wasn't room for a grand piano in the split-level house in the fancy subdivision we moved into, the house with the plate-glass window looking at the fifteenth green.

At first my mother said she had to do something about selling Blacklock, but then she began saying it was a good investment. Uncle Royce was tending the cattle, mowing the lawn with the tractor, and trimming the vines that grew rapidly up the fences, obstructing the view. Eventually she claimed that she was saving Blacklock for Royce to live in when he grew up.

The house at the country club was ordinary but safe, and lightning never struck anywhere near it. Every morning we sat at breakfast staring at the tiny figures of golfers; I think we all felt relieved to have Blacklock and the Posts behind us.

I missed Hope and Glynn, and I know my mother missed Dr. Post, at least at first. Once I heard her crying at night, but I left her alone about it.

She and Dr. Post discussed getting back together, but my mother said she was afraid to live with Hopi, and Hopi's doctor said it was important, when she got out of the hospital, that she live with her father, so, finally, that was that. My mother began to say the whole thing had been a mistake, it had been too soon after my father died for her to remarry, and Dr. Post had never loved her anyway.

Royce wanted to move back to Blacklock, *why* couldn't we move back to Blacklock, but my mother said she was scared out there and it was so much nicer here, with white neighbors and mosquito control.

After a few months Royce began to look cleaner, unlike our cat Eleanor, who stayed wild at the farm. Royce even began to take golf lessons.

I went to see Hopi once at the hospital. She was in the psychiatric ward at the medical university, in a low-security ward where patients were allowed to wear their regular clothes. Hopi had decorated her room with her Indian bedspread and pictures of Kahlil Gibran. She looked fine, although she was wearing that turquoise-and-silver bracelet over the delicate scar around her wrist. In fact, Hopi looked

better than I'd ever seen her. Her eyes were still large as
Bambi's and she had that ginger walk, but her smile was
radiant, maybe from drugs. I wondered what they were giving her and how hard it was to get. "This place," she said,
"is just a country club."

"We're living in a country club too," I said. I knew I didn't
look as happy as Hope did.

"How's your mother?"

"Fine. How's yours?"

She froze, poised as a deer. "You're angry with me."

"Why would I be angry with you? How's Glynn?"

"Glynn's fine," she said.

"I hope you fucking die in here," I said. "I hope you have
a rotten life."

"Don't cry," she said, trying to hug me.

I pushed her away because of the dark that had come up
around me. "I'm okay. I just get real upset sometimes."

We sat and talked for a while and Hope was kind, the way
she'd been kind when I first knew her. We agreed to be
friends no matter what happened, but I knew I'd never be
friends with Hope. The dark was pulling me like a tide,
sucking around my legs. The dark that came up around me
was reddish sometimes, sometimes purplish black. If I didn't
take spirits of ammonia or tranquilizers or steal some alcohol
at night, I couldn't get past the darkness to go to sleep.

"I've taken up painting," I said to Hope. "Momma bought
me all these paints, and an easel."

"That's great to have a hobby," Hope said. "You've always been so creative."

"And I'm writing some poems."

Actually I had painted two pictures and written one poem. The first picture was of a man charred black, walking out of a building engulfed in red flames. The other was a cheerful portrait of Queen Elizabeth, who had turned out to look quite a lot like my mother. I even gave the queen freckles. "Hope, why did you tear up my tiara?"

"Did I do that? I'm sorry. I don't remember much about that night."

"You tore it right up."

"I don't know. Maybe I was trying to protect you. That place out there, Blacklock, it really is weird. Just like you said."

"It's only a place, Hope. Why did you cut up the clothes?"

"There was a ghost out there, Ellen, I swear there was, and it was trying to kill your mother. The clothes were a sacrifice."

Maybe Hopi wasn't as stable as I'd thought. "I think you just hated my mother."

She smiled and shrugged. "That's what the doctors say."

"Did you hate my mother?"

She smiled as if smiling hurt. "They say it's my father I hate."

"Do you hate your father?"

She was fingering the turquoise bracelet. "I really don't know."

When I was leaving, I kissed Hope's smooth white cheek and told her I'd be back, although that was a lie. I gave her my poem and asked her not to read it until I was gone. *For*

Hope, it said, and it began, "Lights flicker and die / in the abandoned house . . ." The last lines were "We are lost / in the night / of life."

Before Mom's divorce was final, she started going out with her lawyer, who had silver hair and looked like a TV star. She began to play a lot of tennis and to have facials. By the time I went to college, she was planning to marry him.

In college I failed calculus, drank too much, and went secretly to civil rights meetings, a habit, which, when my sorority sisters found out, got me in trouble. Antisocial behavior for an Omega, they said. At the end of my sophomore year, when I told the Dean of Students I was quitting school to get married, she said that sounded like a good idea.

On our first date Nicky wore black lace-up shoes like my father's. I kept looking at his feet. I told him my life story while the French restaurant closed up around us. I thought you were a nice girl, Nicky said later, but you talked too much.

On our next date I persuaded him to go to a drive-in to see a horror-movie double feature. I laughed all the way through the first film, something about an Egyptian cult, black cats, sacrifices, and a girl in a bathtub with a knife in her eye. I was drinking straight from a bottle of brandy, so I passed out early in the second movie. When I came to, the other cars were all turning on their headlights and pulling out like a caravan. Nicky and I were still on our mound, with the speaker crackling inside the car window. "This is not," Nicky said, "my idea of fun."

After that, he would not put up with my drinking; when he found me reading a book on witchcraft he threw it away. I was secretly relieved. Nicky did not know about the spirits of ammonia or the tranquilizers, and it didn't seem smart to tell him.

He was completing his Ph.D. and soon had a job at Polaroid, outside of Boston. We rented a large apartment in a brownstone in Back Bay, furnishing it with clean-lined Scandinavian furniture. Having stopped drinking, I took up cooking.

I learned to cook quiche Lorraine and chocolate mousse and creole shrimp and Greek stew. I learned to cook French lamb and minestrone and Polynesian hamburgers. I baked bread and made my own puff pastry. At night I read cookbooks as if they were novels.

I called Nicky "Doc," and in many ways the seven years I spent with him were like a long stay in a good hospital. Nicky supported me financially and emotionally. Success in the world, he kept telling me, was just like cooking. Imagine your goal. Work hard. Think your way through your obstacles.

I understand, I said. Don't aim. Imagine yourself hitting the target.

While I lived with Nicky, the darkness receded. Blacklock and my family began to seem like a dream, or a very funny story. Nicky paid my way through college, taught me to study, and encouraged my interest in social issues. We were liberals, he said, humanists, people with social consciences, and if we were Southerners, well, that was all right, it just meant we understood the plight of minorities with more depth.

After college I got a job as a book editor at a small house in Boston, where I soon developed a reputation for publishing books on civil rights, the antiwar movement, and the women's movement. But I was most pleased by my series of cookbooks, which I knew all had flair, a tinge of outrageousness.

During these years I lost touch with my family, except through phone conversations, brief visits at Christmas, and weddings.

Marie skipped college and married a nice man named Keith who everyone seemed to think was dull; he was a manager for a grocery-store chain called Piggly Wiggly.

My mother buried her third husband, the one with the silver hair. "This one was everything we could have wanted for her," Marie said to me on the phone, "but he just didn't have much staying power."

Royce became a teenager, a clean-cut young man with a good golf game who everyone said had talent as a writer. He edited his school's literary magazine.

Although the schools had been integrated, Marie and Royce were not directly affected because they went to private institutions. The Vietnam War dominated the news, but Royce was too young to be drafted.

The summer he was seventeen, Royce went to work at our father's former business, which had been sold by bank trustees after his death. Royce worked as a field laborer for Skip, who had stayed on as chief foreman for the new owners.

Royce had gotten tall. Marie said he was gangly and awkward; he had started listening to Bob Dylan, the Doors, and the Rolling Stones, and was growing his hair long.

By August, Skip was saying Royce looked like a girl and was threatening to fire him if he didn't cut his hair. Then he began to say that Royce was a peacenik, a draft dodger, and a communist, and if he didn't cut his hair, Skip would hold him down and cut it himself.

"Skip and Royce seem to *hate* each other," my mother told me during a phone update. "Why on *earth* would this happen?"

My mother had gained weight with her third husband and now she was back on diet pills. "Do you think it might be the *heat?* Royce shouldn't be working as a laborer during *August,* he should be out playing golf."

I said I didn't know, because I was busy leaving my husband, or he was busy leaving me, depending on which of us was asked. "You can't leave Nicky," my mother said. "You *adore* Nicky."

But I was drinking again, and I had discovered psychedelic drugs and the antiwar and women's movements in a less than intellectual way. I had decided to leave Nicky and go be a radical.

"Your values are so shallow," I said to my mother. "Royce is growing his hair as a political statement. You people are part of the problem, not part of the solution."

"Royce is growing his hair because he is seventeen years old. What do you mean, *you people?"*

So, the same summer Skip and Royce had their fight, I

moved to a women's commune in Mendocino, California, and while Skip and two other men were holding Royce down on the floor of the warehouse and cutting his long hair, I was probably sitting in a teepee taking acid. I don't actually know what I was doing when Royce pulled the sawed-off broom handle out of his pants—it was my Mom's good broom, the new one—and hit Skip, because I was taking drugs almost every day. The broom handle hit Skip along the side of his head, right below his temple. Skip dropped like dead weight because he was dead.

Since Skip had used a wrench to threaten him, Royce was not prosecuted. The other two men testified on Royce's behalf at the inquest. But my brother was too young to be drafted, and he had killed a man who loved him in a fight.

I did not go home even for this, although I saw Royce's picture in the paper. My mother sent it to me. Royce looked young and sad. His hair was cropped like a soldier's.

I went home four years later, for Royce's wedding, and I took my girlfriend with me.

Royce was marrying a Charleston aristocrat. He had one more year at Duke's engineering school, where I had failed calculus. Royce had stayed out of the war because of his college deferment, and now the war was over. He was planning to start his own business and move back to Blacklock.

"Blacklock?" I kept saying. "Blacklock? You would move back to Blacklock?"

"I was happy there, Ellen," Royce said.

Royce's face had a sadness I tried not to respond to. "What if I wear a tuxedo to your wedding?"

"I don't care what you wear. I'm just glad that you're here."

Royce's wedding took place in the same church where our mother had married Dr. Post, only it was not in the side chapel, and Father Spratt had moved away. Royce's wedding was a major social event with three hundred people attending. My lover and I wore dresses and sat with the family, against my mother's objections, but Royce insisted.

My mother was upset with me because of my tattoo. The tattoo, small and on my shoulder, said RAIN, which I insisted was my new name. A patch of slanted lines was supposed to be some rain falling, but that part hadn't come out so well.

"Your name is Ellen Larraine Burns," my mother said, while we were dressing for the wedding.

"I'm wearing sleeves, Momma, and it's covered up."

My lover, Alex, was leggy and had a mane of red hair. She was, or had been, a news producer for a network affiliate, when I met her at a demonstration in San Francisco. Alex left her husband for me, a fact that I didn't yet know was temporary.

"What is a nice normal girl like *you* doing with *Ellen?*" my mother said to her.

"Momma, those diet pills are bad for you. They make you talk in italics. Did you know you talk in italics?"

"Ellen is a very interesting person," Alex said, "and she's more conventional than she seems."

"Listen, Alexandra," I said, "whose side are you on?" That was her real name, and she hated it.

"There aren't any sides here, Rain." She turned to my mother. "And I think Rain is a beautiful name."

"You should have changed your name to Lightning," my mother said. "What's the matter with Thunder?"

Royce had written the wedding service himself. There was no mention of obeying—he used the word *cherish* instead—and there was a long passage he and his wife read to each other, but I couldn't listen to it because the organist was playing "Born Free" as background music, and Marie and I developed the giggles. Our mother, glittering with intensity, kept staring at us.

Marie had gained some weight. The asthma she'd developed as a child had gotten worse, but she looked happy sitting beside Keith. They'd bought the house our family had lived in before we moved to Blacklock, the small house with one identical to it on every block.

Alex and I visited them there after the wedding reception. We hadn't stayed for the dancing, for which Royce had hired a rock band. "I *hate* to see all the heterosexuals dancing," I said, trying to sound as if I were joking. Marie said she didn't like to dance anyway, and Alex said I was talking in italics, like my mother.

It was odd to be in the house where I'd been a child, before I'd ever heard of Blacklock. Marie's furnishings seemed a lot like the ones we had when we were children. "I feel safe here," Marie said, and then she told me she was pregnant.

When we were in the kitchen alone for a few minutes, she put her arms around me; I could hear the wheeze in her breathing. "You're not this tough, Ellen," she whispered. "It's sad to see you so confused."

I pulled away from her. "I'm not *confused.*"

A few months later, when Alex went back to her husband, I ended up in a psychiatric ward in a private hospital in California.

When I got out I was shaky but okay, as if I'd had successful major surgery. I had been advised not to take any more drugs, which I'd agreed to, and not to drink. I felt less willing about that.

Royce had moved to Blacklock. He had started his own business with some capital from our mother and from his wife's parents and had joined the Yacht Club in Charleston. "He's so pretentious now," Marie told me on the phone. "He actually said to me, 'Mother will never learn to like pâté.' 'Right,' I said, 'because she'll know it's just liver.' "

I moved to Los Angeles, and, after some skidding around, ended up writing for a television parody of soap operas that came on every night at eleven-thirty. "You're very funny," people said to me. "How do you think of these things?"

I made a lot of money, most of which I put up my nose in the form of cocaine. So much for advice from doctors.

Royce was successful in his new business at first, and he began to restore Blacklock. He learned to play Marie's old grand piano by ear, just like our father, using mostly the black keys. He rebuilt the dam, planning to farm shrimp in the rice paddies. He bought horses and built stables. But he had expanded his business too fast, and banks closed in on him. Then his wife left him for their dog trainer. Then our

166

mother, who claimed to be in financial trouble of her own, put Blacklock on the market. She said she needed the cash, but Royce told Marie he thought she was doing it to punish him, because of his business failing, and because of what happened with Skip.

Royce disappeared.

He wasn't there when Blacklock was sold to a group of men who didn't care about the house, who wanted only the land for duck hunting in the paddies. He wasn't there when Marie was hospitalized during her second pregnancy. She'd had a severe asthma attack and nearly died, and there was fear the fetus had been harmed. He wasn't there when her little boy was born and the doctors said he was fine. "Royce may be dead," Marie said to me on the phone, because I was still afraid to go home.

The police looked for Royce, of course. He'd taken his car and a suitcase, but Momma said Royce would never do this to us so there had to be *foul play*. Marie grieved for Royce and kept saying she knew he was dead.

Royce disappeared for four years, and just when I began to think Marie might be right, I got a letter from him. The envelope was addressed to me in care of a company where I no longer worked, and it took a while to find me. "I'm living up in Mendocino County," he wrote, "and I'm fine. I hope you're okay too. I miss you, and I miss home, but I'm never going back. I thought you would understand." Royce had set up shop as a carpenter, and he was living with a woman. They weren't married, but they had a baby daughter.

With his letter Royce included a short story he'd written.

It was handwritten in pencil on blue-lined school paper, and there were many erasures and corrections. He'd drawn little balls on his quotation marks.

John's Song

Galan James stepped onto the oyster-shell drive from the front steps of the old plantation house. The drive circled an oak tree in the yard and ran down the hill, out the old stone gate. Walking up the drive was an old black man in overalls and denim jacket—both worn almost white.

"John Tillman—that looks like John Tillman!" thought Galan. John Tillman was coming up the drive and Galan was grinning as he ran down and shook John's hand.

It was ten years ago that Galan had met John Tillman, when Galan was five years old and John was already ancient. Uncle Winston had hired John to help around the old plantation shortly after Galan's dad was killed in a car accident. Uncle Winston and Aunt Izzie moved into the plantation's guest house because Galan's mom wasn't going to stay alone way out in the country, amid a sea of poor blacks. John cut the grass and fed the horses and cows, and Galan followed him when he worked close to the house. They became friends.

John and his family lived right outside the gate in an old shack with a fireplace. Smoke came from the chimney summer or winter, as they depended on their fire for cooking as well as heating. Ruby, his wife, could be seen every day carrying wood or hanging wash in the dirt-packed backyard of their house. Galan never once had seen the inside of their house, and he was unsure if their son Junior lived there (if he was their son), or if he lived out on the paved road with a relative. There were many

shacks out on the road, several with Tillmans living in them. Junior didn't
seem to be at John's house all that much, and Galan never asked why.

The most incredible thing Galan had ever heard was John's voice. It
was a song straight out of Africa—velvety, rich, and flowing. His eyes
laughed as the sentences ran together without pauses, their lyrics just a
mystery. At five years old Galan just about needed an interpreter to
understand the old black man, and communication from John was mostly
John's demonstrative gestures. Galan recognized few of John's words for
quite a while. Even years later, when John talked his Gullah to other
blacks, he could quicken the tempo, and for Galan the meaning would be
lost in the music of his voice.

One Saturday when Galan was seven, John said they would "Gwine-
fushwidswumeendepon." Only after John had picked up the fishing rod
and dug shrimp from Mom's outside freezer did Galan understand that
they were going fishing with shrimp in the saltwater pond. Galan caught
an eel and John skinned it for him. Mom didn't want it but Galan insisted
it be stored in the freezer as any proper fish should.

In the spring John took his mule and hand plow and tilled Uncle
Winston's garden. "Gup Mule," sang John, and the three of them made
a train in the garden. Galan stepped carefully in John's footprints as
Mule, John, and Galan made long, straight furrows for tomatoes, squash,
cucumbers, and even peanuts. Galan was nonstop with questions as John
listened and did his work, answering only once in a while in a single long
song when an answer was required. They would stop at lunch and Galan
might try to teach John addition and subtraction in the dirt the way his
teacher taught him at school on the blackboard. John would just laugh and
say, "Gwineboy I tole for tawt."

Later years found John skinning a deer for Galan, showing him how
to keep the meat clean by not slicing the intestines and properly cutting

the meat into hams, shoulders, loins, and ribs. Once he showed Galan how to skin an alligator, but Galan would take none of the meat no matter how pretty and white it looked.

The years moved fast and Galan's mom remarried, and the family moved back into town. Uncle Winston moved into the big plantation house and John continued to work for him. Galan was twelve and came out to the plantation seldom, and he never was there when John was around. Girls became more important than Galan ever imagined, and plantation living was like an ended chapter in Galan's life.

And now John Tillman was walking on the oyster-shell road just as he always had. Galan was fifteen. Uncle Winston came out and spoke to John. "You ready?"

"Yahsuhcop'n," said John, and he climbed into the back of Uncle Win's truck.

"You want to go, Galan?" asked Uncle Winston.

"Yes sir," said Galan. "John, do you still have Mule?"

"Yahsuh," said John.

Galan heard something different in John's voice, and the song was suddenly different. Galan was puzzled.

They rode slowly down the road and Galan asked about Ruby and Junior, but John barely answered. Galan tried to rekindle John's song with questions, but the answers were short and he avoided Galan's eyes. They were sitting on the same side of the truck bed, and suddenly John grabbed Galan between the legs and pulled hard.

Galan's right fist caught John just below the eye and he shouted at the same time, "You motherfucker! Are you crazy?"

And John looked at him and laughed. An ugly laugh. Galan looked hard at John's face and eyes and saw the fractured light in them. John

*seemed to be looking at someone over Galan's shoulder and he knew in
that instant that John was crazy. He didn't know how or why, but John
Tillman was crazy, and after that day he never saw John Tillman again.*

*Uncle Winston told him a few months later that Ruby had committed
John to the state mental hospital and had moved away from the shack by
the gate. Junior had moved to another small town to work.*

*Galan heard three years later that John had died in the hospital, and
when Galan returned years later he was drawn down to the old shack.
It was late afternoon in early September. The air around the shack was
thick and warm beneath the big oak tree in the front yard. Galan walked
up onto the porch and looked in the front door and listened . . . and in
his mind he could just hear John's song . . . rich and full and velvet.*

Royce had included his phone number but no address. I
didn't call before I went up to Mendocino County to find
him. He'd said he didn't want Momma and Marie to know
that he was alive, and I wanted to argue with him about that.

After some trouble I found him. He was living in a small
cabin without electricity or running water on a cliff over-
looking the ocean. The woman with him was Vietnamese. "I
am happy to meet you," she said to me in careful, perfect
English. "Royce is a good writer, yes?"

"Yes," I said.

Her name was Santane. She was remarkably beautiful and
shy, and while I was there she spent most of her time taking
care of their infant daughter, who was named Ruby.

"Did you make the story up?" I asked him. We were

sitting outside on the edge of the cliff, and I was drinking from a bottle of Jack Daniel's I'd brought as a present. Royce was drinking tea. "I'm a Buddhist now, sort of. I try, anyway. So I don't drink or anything like that."

Royce's chest had filled out, and he'd grown a beard. He looked wild, the way he had as a child, except for his eyes, which were extraordinarily calm. "The story is not factual," he said after thinking about my question. "The events are altered, and some are made up. But it's as true as I know how to make it. Do you understand?"

"I understand," I said.

After some discussion, Royce agreed to contact Momma and Marie himself, and a few weeks later he did. He talked to each of them on the phone several times, but he did not go back home.

There's not much else to tell about Blacklock except that, two years after Royce reappeared, I went to a party there.

I had become a book editor again and was living in Boston, but several of my old television friends had stayed in touch. One of them, Tyler Jones, was scouting locations for a film that was to be shot mostly on a plantation near Charleston named Boone Hall. Boone Hall had previously been Twelve Oaks in *Gone With the Wind.*

Tyler called and asked me to come down to Charleston. "I'll make you a story consultant. This place is such a trip. Did you really grow up here?"

"Some people would argue that I never grew up, that I'm having the world's longest adolescence." But I took a few days of vacation time and flew home.

Tyler, who was black and gay, had grown up in the Bronx. He was an elegant dresser and spoke white English perfectly. "Learned it from TV." He said he liked the South because he felt instinctively comfortable there, just as he did with displaced Southerners like me.

I made an obligatory stop at my mother's condominium but thought it wiser not to take Tyler with me. "Can you believe that Royce has married an Oriental?" my mother said.

"Well, he isn't exactly married to her, Mom. I'm not sure he got divorced from his first wife."

Mom was looking better with some weight on her, but she'd frosted her hair, which made her face look old. "What does his baby look like, Ellen? Is she . . . dark? Is that why he named her Ruby?"

"It's a nice name," I said.

From Mom's I called Marie to say hello and to tell her I'd be by her house first thing tomorrow. "I've got somebody I want to introduce you to."

Late the next morning Tyler and I took a carriage tour around the old part of Charleston. He had a shoulder-mounted camera and was shooting footage everywhere we went. He shot the cannons on the Battery and the fancy houses from which residents had watched the firing on Fort Sumter, which had begun the Civil War. He shot the graceful moss-hung oaks in White Point Park. He shot the leather diaper on the horse that pulled our carriage.

In the afternoon we drove out to Folly Beach and had drinks in a restaurant sitting out in the surf on spindly pilings, one of two houses left from the front row. "The houses here were destroyed in the hurricane of 1938," I told Tyler.

"You drink too much, honey, you know that?" Tyler was shorter than me, a burly, robust man. He was eating boiled shrimp and drinking a glass of white wine. I'd had two quick Jack Daniel's and was nursing a third.

"I've got no excuses."

"Don't get drunk, my friend. I've got plans for us tonight. You know what an oyster roast is?"

"Of course I know what an oyster roast is." I was watching the waves breaking under us.

"When we were scouting plantations I found this weird old place with hippies living in it, and they invited me to this oyster roast tonight. You interested?"

"Where is it?"

"It's an old plantation called Blacklock. Out south of Charleston."

"Blacklock?" I said. "Blacklock?"

"Jesus, Ellen, take it easy."

"There are hippies living in it?"

"I met two of them, but I guess there's maybe five or six. I met a boy named Maurice and his girlfriend, Hilton. The boy seemed freaked out, but then his girlfriend told me his parents had died in a murder-suicide pact. Can you beat that?"

"Oh, yes, I can beat that." I was already on my feet, throwing money on the table.

"Ellen, what is it? What is Blacklock?"

"My home," I said.

October is a mild, bright month in South Carolina. The humidity drops, the few deciduous trees lose their leaves, and the green of the live oaks and the pines becomes more vivid.

Tyler and I got out to Blacklock as the light was failing, but I could see that Ruby and John Tillman's shack was gone. Where it had been was a shallow, burned-out crater.

The big green gate had been taken off its hinges and was lying in the marsh.

The whiteness of the oyster-shell drive had faded away; it looked like any other dirt road.

Vines had grown up over all the fences, closing off the view of the pasture in front of the house and the rice paddies behind it. Only the two acres of lawn around the house were still clear. The woods seemed to be closing in on Blacklock. I was surprised that the giant oak in the front yard, the one split during the hurricane, was still alive.

Tyler recorded all of this for me with his camera. "You could shoot one hell of a horror movie out here," he said.

"Or something," I said.

Tyler was being careful with me, but I had gotten control of myself. Maurice and Hilton showed us around the house, which they were renting from the men who hunted ducks

in the rice fields. Outside, party guests were arriving in beat-
up cars.

My mother's burgundy velvet curtains were still hanging
in the living room, but they were in tatters; the sheers were
gray and rotten. Her chandeliers were burning, and the
wooden floor still shone, but a small patch had been eaten
through by termites.

One end of the living room held dirty wicker furniture,
and the other end contained a hutch with three rabbits in it.
There was newspaper spread under the wire cage, but rabbit
droppings were scattered across the floor.

Above the double fireplace were blank spots, where my
parents' portraits had been.

"I can't *believe* you used to live here," said Maurice, who
had brown hair and a bad complexion. He was smoking a
joint and offered me a hit. "What was it like? We always
wondered who lived here."

Against my better judgment I smoked the dope. Tyler
frowned at me.

Hilton's blond hair was in two long pigtails. She smiled as
if she were afraid.

"How come you keep rabbits in the living room?" I
asked.

"Oh, we're going to move them out soon," Hilton said.
"We only got them a few weeks ago. They seemed real
nervous."

"I'll bet." I could feel the mellowing and spinning of the
dope. "This place is kind of scary, don't you think?"

Hilton hesitated, then spoke in a rush. "When we first

moved in, we put salt in all the rooms. I heard somewhere
that salt helps."

"Salt?"

"It's religious. For the spirits, you know?"

Tyler had turned on the camera. "Do you mind?" He was
pretending to film the room, but I understood that he was
trying to record them too.

"One day I was here by myself and I got real scared,"
Hilton said, still smiling in that frightened way. "There was
this weird feeling in the air, so I just went into the hall and
shouted, 'We live here too! We don't care if you live here,
but we live here too!' After that it was better, you know? It
feels pretty good here now, most of the time."

"Whose piano is that out on the porch?" Maurice said. "It
doesn't play anymore because it got water in it when the
pipe upstairs broke."

"It was my sister's."

"Did your mother paint those bathrooms upstairs pink
and blue? Sometimes we get high and just go look at those
bathrooms."

Later, very drunk, I sat by myself on the front steps, feeling
philosophical. A lot of things had not happened yet. Marie
was still alive, and Royce had not published his novel. I had
not gotten sober or met Meg. Marie was still alive. So I was
just sitting there watching the party and thinking about how
I was free of Blacklock, and of South Carolina.

There were trestle tables set up under the big oak; nearby

was a fire pit covered with a big sheet of iron, where the oysters were being roasted. Tyler had given up trying to film because it had gotten too dark, but I had shown him how to use the special glove and knife, and he'd been standing at one of the tables eating the hot oysters for almost an hour. "Aren't you doing this?" he called to me.

"As God is my witness," I called back, "I'll never be hungry again!"

Earlier, with Maurice, I'd gone upstairs to see the bathrooms. The pink and blue paint had turned bright and overpowering. Inside the cabinet door beneath the sink I found the place where I'd written in pencil *Daddy died, Feb. 21, 1957.* Someone had placed a small mound of salt beneath it.

I'd asked Maurice about the abandoned house out near the graveyard and he'd said there wasn't any house out there, it was just woods. I'd asked him about the Tillman shack's being burned, but he said that had happened before they moved in. I asked if his parents had died *after* he'd moved out here, and he said yes. "I'll give you my best advice, Maurice. This is not a good place to live."

People had begun pulling their cars up and leaving their headlights on, trying to light the trestle tables.

Hilton came to sit beside me on the steps. "It's so dark here," she said, smiling.

"I always said, nobody's ever going to know what happened at Blacklock." I was thinking of the abandoned house out in the pasture, and of the graveyard, and I was speaking carefully, so I wouldn't slur my words. "Y'all don't even know about the lights, do you?"

"What lights?"

Vines had grown up over everything. Maybe the bulbs had burnt out, or the wiring had rotted. "I'll go see."

I stumbled into the hallway and opened the door to the haunted closet under the stairs. The switch was there. When I went back out onto the porch, Blacklock was flooded with light.

Chapter 8

When my mother asked me to come home and take care of her during her facelift, Meg didn't want me to go. "First of all, this is your home now, not Charleston. Second of all, I'm worried about you."

We had just bought our house in Vermont, a wonderful house with huge granite outcroppings behind it. Plate-glass windows across the front stare at a river. "You buy the house," Meg said, the first day we looked at the property. "I'm buying the rocks."

Meg is rock crazy, and our living room contains a long shelf of rocks she claims talk to her. Meg, who was beaten as a child, says that from rocks she learned to be quiet. "Cigar-store Indian," her mother called her, but the violence in her home was rarely directed at Meg. I like picturing her at nine or ten, skating around Los Angeles, her braids flying behind her, finding her stony companions and lugging them back to her room.

The first time Meg invited me to have dinner at her apartment, she held up a clay-colored rock that reminded me of a loaf of bread. "I found this one in Venice," she said, "the first time my mother tried to kill herself."

Meg was not quiet that night. She went through each rock, explaining, but I was too flustered to listen. I already knew that Meg's mother had been a minor movie star, her father a studio publicist, and that they got married on Cary Grant's yacht. The rocks just looked like rocks to me.

I was thinking that Meg did look like an American Indian, because of the long black braid. Her eyes seemed faintly Chinese. She was slight, but her forearms were heavily muscled, like a man's. She did not look to me like the daughter of a minor movie star. I kept staring at her forearms. "Your arms are remarkable," I said.

Some people don't understand sexuality between women. I don't claim to either. "But what do you *do?*" my mother once asked me.

"You mean in bed?"

My mother was looking jowly, and she'd just dyed her hair a reddish brown.

I thought her question over, wondering whether she really wanted an answer. "Nothing much. We hold hands. Stuff like that."

The giant gold tooth of pyrite and the quartz crystal the size of a football that rest in the center of Meg's rock shelf belong to me. "I guess I'm not subtle," I said when I brought these objects back from Peru.

It was because of Peru that Meg didn't want me to take care of my mother during her facelift. "You just seem kind of crazy since you got back."

"You talk to rocks and you think I'm crazy." But Meg is a psychology professor, and she doesn't use words like *crazy* casually.

I'd gone to Peru to be initiated by a shaman, and, in the three months since my return, I'd been pursued by a group of imaginary little girls. "Some people get in touch with their inner child," Meg said. "You have to get a crowd."

"So I'm extreme."

I ended up in Peru through a series of accidents. When I met Meg, I was working as a book editor, and a cookbook I'd just written turned out to be a best-seller. *How to Cook Redneck* was a joke, really. It contained recipes like Hog's Head Cheese—"Take one half hog's head. Boil till soft . . ."—and recommended cooking green beans "till soft and slightly burnt. Should be crusty on bottom, with fatback disintegrated into gummy little pieces." Many of the recipes were quite good, except for Hog's Head Cheese, which I would not eat under any circumstances.

Because of the cookbook I began to get magazine assignments, and I quit my job because I could. The offers I was getting were too interesting—skydiving, Iceland, Thailand—and a studio even hired me to write a screenplay. The screenplay developed a small reputation: unproducible but hilarious. Movie producers continued to court me.

"My life has gotten very strange since I met you," I said to Meg when we were in Iceland, on the Mid-Atlantic Ridge, at a place where the skin of the earth is only inches deep and huge mud pots boil through the surface.

"You seem normal enough to me. Your life was strange before I met you."

Meg is tenured and unfirable, so she has a license to be eccentric as well as lots of free time. "There's nothing wrong with you, Ellen," she said one night when we were staying at the Beverly Wilshire, "except that you're so alive."

Neither of us liked the Beverly Wilshire—too artificial, and L.A. was upsetting to Meg in general—so the producer I was negotiating with gave us his beach house in the Malibu Colony for a week. There was no room service, but we lounged in the hot tub and watched the waves breaking on the beach. I saw Larry Hagman taking a walk one morning, Linda Ronstadt the same afternoon. "I could get used to this," I said. Actually, my skin was getting weird from the chlorine in the hot tub, and from the persistent sun.

"No, you couldn't," Meg said. "You'd be bored to death. We both prefer the bleak and difficult East."

Meg and I stayed in L.A. for ten days, and she drove me to the Santa Monica neighborhood where she'd grown up. A fashionable Cajun restaurant had replaced her house. Her father was in a nursing home nearby, but we didn't go see him. Her mother had died ten years ago of an overdose.

Meg is puzzled and troubled by my obsession with my past. "You haven't lived in South Carolina for twenty years, but it's always in your mind."

"Not always."

"Always."

When we bought the house in Vermont, we began trying to make a home for ourselves. Immediately we had trouble. Neither of us had lived with anyone in years, so we each had our own silverware and plates, and we didn't know which to use. We weren't sure who should cut the grass. I liked to cook and Meg didn't, and was that a bad pattern?

Meg and I met in Alcoholics Anonymous.

When I had been sober for three years, I started going to a women's meeting in Cambridge. The meeting was called "After Three," and it was geared for women who'd been in the program awhile. Meg didn't say much in these meetings, but what she said was interesting. There was a composure about her that I liked. Her words had an aphoristic quality. "I'm a happy person," she liked to say, "except when I'm not."

We started playing racquetball together, and I saw her arms. I saw her legs. One day, as we were dressing to play, I saw her naked back. Her body was precisely muscled, like an anatomy drawing. "Do you work out with weights?"

"I swim every day, and I don't eat much fat."

I knew when she asked me to dinner that she had decided to go to bed with me.

During the years I was drinking, I'd had several lesbian relationships I'd thought were important. Sober, I was beginning to think that my attractions to women were merely a symptom of my alcoholism. Then I met Meg.

Meg was showing me her rocks when I said, "I've never done this sober."

"Done this?" Her eyes changed and I saw that she understood. I wished she would laugh. She put down the rock she was holding, and I actually felt as if I might faint. "Oh, well," I said.

"Sex is a state, Ellen," Meg said quietly, "not an act. If you think it's an act, you'll miss it."

I had the sensation of moving through water. There was a lassitude that made my arms and legs heavy. When I leaned against her, she put her arms around me. Some people think there is a central pulse in the world, a core beat. I had not understood that notion before. "Do you feel that?" I said.

She nodded, and I felt her trembling. "Slow," she said. "Slow."

I had felt physical transformations before: on LSD and other mind-altering drugs, and at the ashram after Rama struck me on the forehead, but I had never experienced what happened to me with Meg. She was rough sometimes, and I was too. Sometimes she sucked my breasts so hard I cried. Because of my uncle, I get easily afraid. "Breasts are made for this," she whispered. "I won't hurt you." We both got scratched and bruised, but sometimes we were so gentle I drifted out of myself and could not distinguish my body from hers.

I saw visions making love with Meg, dark, swimming images of boys I'd been attracted to, women I'd thought I'd wanted, and people I'd never seen before: a man staring up at me through water, androgynous children with wise faces. Once I saw a landscape like a desert, with high, reddish stone pillars in it. "I think I just saw another world, Meg. Another planet or something." I wanted to describe it to her, the strange light, the sensation that I was flying. "I hope I'll always remember that this happened."

"You'll remember."

"I hope so."

She had sat up and was lighting a cigarette. There was still sweat across her shoulders, a flush above her breasts.

"Sometimes I can't believe you still do something so unhealthy to your body."

"You say things like that a lot. That you hope you'll remember this or that. Like you think you're going to lose something."

"You're just so careful with yourself otherwise."

"Ellen, I'm dealing with my addictions in the order that they're killing me. Smoking hasn't cost me enough yet. Why do you think you'll lose this too?"

"I don't know if that's what I'm saying."

Soon after that, I began to cry whenever we made love. At first Meg was kind. "Just don't stop," I'd say, "just please don't stop."

"You're the one who's stopping, Ellen, with all this crying."

But there was an inaccessibility about Meg that troubled me, something I couldn't get to. She said, when I tried to explain, "Maybe you mean my adulthood."

"I mean something else."

"You mean cigar-store?"

"No," I said, though I wondered if I did. Maybe the very

quality that had drawn me to Meg was what I was now resenting.

I felt Meg's withdrawal from me begin, then accelerate. "I think you're creating it," she said. "There's a kind of black hole in you I can't possibly fill. When you reach for me, it feels as if you're actually pushing me away."

"That sounds like shrink talk, Meg."

"You're just so hungry."

"Is that bad?"

"It is if nothing I can do is enough for you."

The first of the imaginary children appeared to me in a dream. The shaman was lying on the porch of my mother's beach house, on a chaise longue with a beach towel over his belly. He looked pregnant. "Don't you want to see her?" he said. "Don't you even want to see her?"

"No, I certainly don't." I had started to leave when a little girl came through the door to the kitchen. She was maybe five or six years old, fat, with blond greasy hair, and she was wearing my little white dress. Her eyes were crusted over, and she tapped the floor in front of her with a long red cane.

The shaman spit on me, a misty stream of Tabu perfume. "Take her with you," he said.

Then the little girl and I were in my Jaguar, and we were driving to Burger King. She began to hit me with the cane. Her eyes were open and red with hate. The blindness had been a trick. "I'm your appetites," she whispered fiercely, "and you'll never get away from me."

The last thing I remember is that she was eating a small mountain of cheeseburgers, one after another, and vomiting them back up on the floor of my car.

I awoke from this dream in our living room, not in bed. I was soaked with sweat, and I'd poured a jar of Planter's peanuts into a small mountain on the glass-topped coffee table. My mouth felt dry and pasty with nuts.

"Ellen?" Meg was standing in the doorway behind me. She was wearing the red silk robe I'd given her when we were in Thailand. "What's the matter?"

"I guess I'm too hungry," I said.

I bought the Jaguar because of the shaman. His name was Don Eduardo, and several books had been written about him, which I hadn't bothered to find out before I went to Peru. I wasn't really a journalist, though people kept treating me like one.

The shaman was a small, beetlelike man with a thick black mustache that curved down around his mouth. He wore his black hair in a ponytail. He spoke only Spanish, but the anthropologist who had organized the trip translated.

The shaman talked a lot about "power animals," archetypal sources with which the initiate must develop relationships. He said there were four cardinal power animals: the snake, the horse, the eagle, and the jaguar. Of these, the jaguar was the most important.

"I don't think he meant a car," Meg said.

"I know that." But I could offer no other explanation for why I'd bought an automobile I didn't trust and couldn't afford.

"It takes three people to make a Jaguar," Meg said. "One to build the car, one to hold the candle, and one to dance around it singing the incantations." She held her arms up and waved them around.

But Meg admitted she liked the leather seats and the wal-nut-burl dashboard. "It's a very sexy automobile."

"You have no idea how much dancing around and singing incantations I did just like that in Peru. It looked a lot like that."

The anthropologist had organized a group of Americans into a kind of New Age comedy to reenact the entire sha-manic initiation in only two weeks, a process that ordinarily takes years. I did think it would make a very funny article.

The first night of ceremonies took place in the Nazca Plains. On the desert at Nazca, huge figures are drawn across the earth. These figures—among them a monkey, a spider, and even a whale—are visible only from the air, which has led to much rather silly speculation that they are related to visitors from outer space. The figures are, however, quite old. They date from the fifth to the fifteenth century, and their origins and purposes are obscure.

At midnight we entered a figure called the Needle and Thread, a long thin triangle with a spiral at its base. After chanting and drinking sacred potions, we were to walk, one by one, into the spiral. The spiral was doubled, turning back in on itself at its center, so by walking in, we would walk back out.

It was pitch dark, and I was a little spooked by the chanting, and by the fervor of the other participants. They had all drunk Don Eduardo's potion, which contained, according to the anthropologist, a psychotropic cactus unclassified in the West. Being a member of A.A., I had decided to take my mysticism straight.

"Don't you see the jaguar?" one woman said to me, pointing into the darkness.

"I don't do drugs anymore." When it was my turn to enter the spiral, I sauntered in.

Immediately I was nervous. I concentrated on the vague outline of the path. In a dozen steps the path began to disappear. I could hear my own breathing, and I felt something catlike in my shoulders. My legs felt like haunches. I began to see clearly, and I walked the dark path easily. I suppressed the desire to roar.

At breakfast the next morning I told the anthropologist what I'd experienced. He told Don Eduardo, who stared hard at me for several seconds, then said something rapidly.

"Don Eduardo says that perhaps you are afraid of your sexuality."

The anthropologist was boyishly good-looking, and he enjoyed telling me this.

"Isn't everybody?" I said.

The anthropologist translated again. "Don Eduardo says no, and that he has twelve children."

"Tell him maybe his wife should be afraid of her sexuality."

Apparently Don Eduardo understood English even though he didn't speak it, because he laughed out loud.

The second child appeared to me at breakfast with Meg. We were sitting at the dining-room table, eating my special granola. Light glittered on the river. Out of the corner of my eye I saw a child staring at me. She was sitting right at the table with us, and in front of her was an empty bowl. This one was maybe seven or eight years old. She was wearing a Supergirl suit of red, white, and blue, decorated with stars. A blue towel was tied around her neck, in imitation of a cape. Her hair was set in ringlets, like Little Lulu's. I could remember Little Lulu from comic books when I was a child. I had never liked Little Lulu. "You look absurd in that outfit," I said, "especially with your hair like that."

Meg's spoon stopped in midair. She was wearing a green Chinese robe with a large pink poppy embroidered on the back. Her black hair was not braided but hung loose down her back. "What's the matter with my hair?" she said.

Through the doorway to the bedrooms came the little blind girl, tapping her cane. "She's not really blind," I said to Meg. "It's an act."

Comprehension appeared in Meg's eyes, then relief, then alarm. "The child you saw in your dream?"

"Meg," I said, "what's the difference between a vision and a hallucination? Do you think there is one?"

"Well," Meg said, as if this were an entirely ordinary conversation, "if I thought this granola was a steak, that's a hallucination. A vision is superimposed over reality. I mean, you can tell it's not real."

Meg likes my granola. It's a recipe I made up, and it's not in *How to Cook Redneck.*

"Suppose I told you there's a little girl sitting here with us and she's wearing a Supergirl suit."

"Are they talking to you yet?"

"No."

There was a long silence. "I'd say you shouldn't have gone to Peru."

I got a Jungian analyst to help me with the kids. Meg recommended a Jungian because "a Jungian might know what to do with this. Maybe you got some kind of drug you didn't know about. I don't think you're schizophrenic."

"Thanks a lot, Meg."

Dr. Bonner was a nice gray-haired lady wearing a flowery print dress. Her eyebrows were gray too, and looked as if she combed them. "I'm a recovering alcoholic," I told her. "I'm also an editor, a screenwriter, a journalist, a lesbian, and a very good cook. Probably in that order. Do you mind?"

"Should I?" Dr. Bonner said.

"I went to Peru and apparently I've gotten myself in some sort of trouble."

Dr. Bonner didn't seem worried. She said the children were unrealized projections of myself; she said they were unintegrated material; she said they were messages from my unconscious. She said I was lucky.

"But what are they *doing* here?"

"Why don't we ask them?"

We set up some chairs where the imaginary children were supposed to sit, but of course they didn't want to. Supergirl sat on top of the lamp on Dr. Bonner's desk. The bulimic went through the trashcan, where she found a chocolate-bar wrapper and ate it. A piece of tinfoil stuck to her lip.

The two of them wouldn't talk to me or to Dr. Bonner, but it was at her office that the third one presented herself. In one of the chairs appeared a little girl who was horribly burned. Her face and hands were a net of scars. She was wearing a long black cape. I cried when I saw her, and Dr. Bonner said that was good.

"You think everything is good," I said, sniffing.

The little girl with the scars said, "Watch me, watch me," and, when I did, she turned herself into a cone of light. "I can do magic tricks," she said, reappearing in her black cape. She began to shudder, and once again she turned into a cone of light.

Dr. Bonner said this girl represented my sexuality and creativity; the bulimic one represented some place of starvation in me, probably for my mother; Supergirl was who I wished I was.

"You think I *want* to look like Little Lulu? Why does

everyone keep mentioning sex, am I giving off some kind of aura? Anyway, I like my mother."

"Ah, your mother," Dr. Bonner said. "We'll talk about her next time."

But there wasn't going to be a next time, because my mother had asked me to come back to South Carolina and take care of her during her facelift. Given the timing, agreeing to her request seemed both complicated and unwise. "I'm working real hard right now," I said into the phone receiver. It felt odd to me that I could speak to the receiver and somehow it was my mother.

"Ellen Larraine, I don't ask you for many things, and I need you to be here. There's nobody you can trust like your own family."

"Mom, I'm not so sure that's true."

On the plane flying home, the world was like a veil that had torn. I believed it was the East Coast below me, and that there were clouds, and I believed the metal skin of the plane would hold me in midair, but these facts seemed to rely on my agreement in some way. My agreement was slipping.

The little girls liked flying, but the bulimic insisted I order two lunches. "I'm pregnant," I said to the stewardess. "Maybe triplets."

At the airport, before my mother arrived to pick me up, I called Meg. "Everything looks kind of translucent. It's like the world is flat, like a picture, and I can see through it."

"Oh, honey," Meg said.

"It's pretty. Really." Meg had probably never said something like "Oh, honey" in her life.

My mother arrived wearing a red sweatsuit that clashed with her hair. "Aren't these *great?*" she said, hugging me. "I bought every color: blue, black, yellow, pink, red, and taupe. Some others I can't remember. Taupe is a kind of gray. Did you know that?"

"I knew that," I said.

My first literary effort, in the third grade, was a poem for my mother. I cut a heart out of red construction paper and put my thumbprint on one side. On the other side I wrote:

> *When we're watching TV*
> *And you're in your seat*
> *You're always nice enough*
> *To get me something to eat.*

Under the poem I glued a cutout picture of Little Debbie, the girl on the boxes of Little Debbie Snack Cakes. I took a Little Debbie Snack Cake to school almost every day in my lunch box. Under the picture of Little Debbie I wrote, *I love you, Mom, Ellen Larraine.*

"I'm the one who wrote that," the blind, bulimic kid said. She bared her teeth at my mother's knee, as if to bite her.

"Stop that," I said.

"Stop what?" my mother said.

"Stop . . . picking your thumb." My mother and I both peel our thumbnails and make them bleed. Genetic memory, perhaps, or a way of being close. Maybe just a shared bad habit.

"Oh, that. I'm doing better."

We held out our thumbs and compared them. My

mother's thumbnails were almost normal length, although they were ridged and thick. Mine were torn out at the beds and rimmed with dried blood.

"Oh, honey," my mother said. "I thought you'd quit that."

"I'm dealing with my addictions in the order that they're killing me. Why is everybody calling me honey?"

"How about sugar pie?" she said, giggling.

I remembered why I liked my mother, and I hugged her again. "I'm glad to be home. I mean, back in Charleston."

Supergirl was holding her hands up for me to inspect her thumbs too, but I wouldn't look at them. "I'm starting to like your outfit," I said aloud. "I don't know about that hair."

My mother looked stricken. "I have to have it this way because I'm going to have little scars behind my ears."

I realized I was going to have to find a way to stop talking to the girls out loud. I looked around for the burn victim. She looked happy, riding the luggage conveyor. She pulled her scarred hand from under her cape and waved. I waved back.

My mother looked over at the luggage. "Ellen Larraine, are you all right?"

"I'm fine. Overworked."

My mother had already told me she wanted a facelift because "Sixty is too young to stop living, and any man old enough for me I'm too old for. You know what I mean?" But one of the characteristics of my mother's age is that she often tells me the same things more than once, in exactly the same words. As we drove in her old Mercedes through North

Charleston, an industrial area of factories and small houses and fast-food places, she repeated her reasons, verbatim.

Two of the kids were riding in the back seat, but the burned one was in the trunk with the luggage. She'd winked at me as she climbed in, and I saw that her eyes were an astounding blue. Her nose and lips and eyebrows were mostly burned away. I spoke to her mentally—*you don't look so bad to me*—and her eyes shone with tears.

"Ellen Larraine, you don't think I ought to do this, do you?"

"I think you've earned your face, and you ought to keep it."

"You'll feel different when you're older."

"Maybe."

My mother lives in a high-rise condominium with guards at the gates and a code to open the front door. "I don't ever want to feel afraid at night," she said. "I'm a woman living alone, and I've been afraid enough in my life."

The first thing I always do at my mother's house is look in the refrigerator. However, my mother has developed some odd patterns in the last ten years, and one is that she doesn't throw old food away. A jar of mayonnaise might have an expiration date two years old. Peanut butter can have a thick, rich crust of mold. Some of the food in the freezer, I suspect, is left over from my childhood. When I'm at my mother's, I worry about botulism.

I opened the refrigerator. There was an open half gallon of cheap white wine on the top shelf. The wine had turned

197

brownish and had a yellow sediment. "What kind of antiques are you keeping in here?" I pulled out the bottle to show her.

"Honey, you left that here. I wouldn't presume to throw your things away."

"Mom, I haven't had a drink in almost five years. We'll just throw it away, okay?"

I closed the refrigerator, and we went out to dinner at a cafeteria we both like.

"A last meal," my mother said. "I bet I won't want to eat tomorrow. Maybe I'll lose some weight."

My mother has dieted her way to being rotund. "You could get in an automobile accident or get a rare disease," I said, "and then you'd lose some weight."

She giggled again. "Want to lose ten ugly pounds? Cut off your head." She'd finished her fried chicken and had started on her strawberry shortcake. I was eating shortcake too, but no matter what I eat, I don't gain weight. That's my father's side of the family.

We went back to her condo and watched TV. Meg's mother appeared briefly in a colorized version of an old movie starring Rosalind Russell. "There's Meg's mother," I said.

"I hate it when you talk about Meg."

"I didn't know I was talking about Meg."

The next morning I dropped my mother off at her doctor's office. He was doing the surgery in his office because, my mother said, that was safer than running the possibility of being interrupted by some emergency at a hospital. This sounded plausible enough to me.

While my mother was having her operation, I took the kids to the beach. I've always loved the Isle of Palms because it's undramatic. The sand is not white, and the water is not aquamarine. The sand is bluish, the waves small, the water tepid. The kids thought it was dull.

I got sunburned, ate a hot dog, and worried about my mind. My sense of translucence was still there, but it was intermittent. Gradually, I felt as if I were waking up. It was the kids who began to seem transparent. Some of the time I couldn't even see them. Maybe this was all just an acid flashback. I hadn't done any acid in ten or fifteen years, but this explanation seemed as likely as any other. Or maybe I just had an overactive imagination, the way my mother had always claimed.

Feeling refreshed and relieved, I went to pick her up at five o'clock. "Don't be too shocked," the doctor said.

My mother was lying propped up and strapped to a table in her blue sweatsuit. She looked unconscious. Her head was swathed in a turban of white bandages. Cotton batting under the tape made her head the size of a watermelon, and only her eyes and nose and mouth were visible. Out of the top of her head ran two thin plastic tubes, like bug feelers.

The kids were suddenly back with me, vivid and loud, running around the office making sounds like *aghhhhgh,* even the burned one.

"Stop that," I said.

The doctor looked at me quizzically. He was a blond young man with a nice face, or maybe he'd had plastic surgery. "She's still out of it from the anesthetic," he said. "She won't even remember you taking her home. Be careful with her in the car. A nurse will be at your house within an hour."

"At her house," I said. "Her condo. I live in Vermont. What are those bug feelers?"

He laughed fondly and touched the plastic tubes coming out of my mother's head. "Let's sit up." He raised her to a sitting position. "You're going home now. Your daughter is here."

My mother was sitting halfway up and staring around wildly.

"Those are blood drains," the doctor said. He unzipped the front of her sweatsuit and showed me a white plastic hand-grenade-shaped object that the tiny tubes emptied into. The hand grenade had been fastened to her brassiere with a safety pin. Her bra was on inside out, which I knew would upset her if she were conscious. "The tubes run under the skin of her face, which you can't see because of the bandages. It's to keep her from swelling or bruising too much." He touched the grenade, which contained half an inch of bloody fluid. "If she doesn't behave, you can pull her around with this."

"That's very funny," I said, to compensate for the fact that I didn't feel like laughing.

A nurse helped me get her into the Mercedes. We couldn't get her seatbelt around her, so at every traffic light I had to put my arm across her chest to keep her head off the dash-

board. The only thing she said on the ride home was "I wish
I was dead."

"No you don't," I said, without conviction.

Awkwardly I managed to park the car and walk her to the
elevator. When we got to her apartment I had to lean her
against the wall while I opened the door. She let me lead her
to her bed. The doctor had said to pile up pillows against the
headboard. For the next few days, it was necessary for her
to sleep sitting up.

I took off her sneakers and got her arranged on the pillows.
Then I brought her some juice to sip through a straw. She
didn't want it. "Get the camera," she mumbled.

"What?"

"Get the camera."

I glanced quickly around the room. There was a Polaroid
on her dresser.

"You want me to take your picture?"

She nodded slightly, painfully.

I took six shots of her in her turban and tubes. For the last
one she fumbled with her sweatsuit and managed to unzip
it. Like Clark Kent exposing his Superman chest, she pulled
it open to display the blood drain.

"Wrong the way you are," she managed to say.

"What?"

"Sober. Still gay. Wrong."

I put the camera on the dresser. "You cut me to the heart,
Mom. Wrong the way you are too."

I sat in the armchair by the window and waited for the
nurse. I was shaking and trying not to think about the cabi-

netful of good bourbon in the living room. It would be so easy. Instead I tried to call Meg, who wasn't home. I left a message on her machine. "I'm okay," I lied. "Everything is fine."

I went back to my mother's room and sat in the armchair by her bed again.

The last day I was in Peru, when we had the final shamanic initiation, Don Eduardo had performed a ceremony to sever our connection to our maternal mothers and reconnect us with the mother earth. We were under a white tropic sun, on a beach near Trujillo, at some supposedly sacred lagoons. To me the lagoons just looked like mud flats. Don Eduardo said the water in this lagoon was supposed to come from the center of the earth, but I thought what we were looking at was merely a gully that had gotten separated from the ocean.

About fifty feet out in the water, the shaman had placed a rudimentary wooden cross.

We were all naked, and, despite sunblock cream, I was getting sunburned on my ass. At his instruction we had each taken a coin and a piece of our hair and wrapped them in cloth strips. "A sacrifice," he said, "of your physical bodies and your attachment to wealth." One by one he had us suck on pieces of lemon that had been soaked in sugar, "to embrace the sweetness and bitterness of life."

When it was my turn for the initiation, I walked out into the water to the cross, immersed myself, stood up, and threw my cloth package. He had said to make a prayer. If I didn't take the shaman seriously I do take prayer that way, so I carefully asked the god of my understanding for wisdom and acceptance, and to keep me sober, no matter what.

Back on the muddy beach, Don Eduardo had drawn a large circle. We stood beside the circle and he spit something sweet-smelling on me, to purify me. Then he took a large old sword with a brass handle and passed it methodically over my "energy body," inches from my skin. I could feel the sword moving down my back and legs, my shoulders and chest and pelvis. "You are severed from your mother now," he said. "Reconnect yourself to the earth."

I rolled in the circle he had drawn on the ground until I was smeared dark, and then I went back into the lagoon and washed, but I could not shake the feeling of absurdity.

Now I was sitting in my mother's condominium in Charleston, South Carolina, and she was lying semiconscious in her white helmet with her blood-drain feelers, and the same sense of absurdity was back. I would always want my mother's approval. I would always feel starved in some way I couldn't name.

"You don't understand."

The burned girl was standing in front of me in her dark cloak, staring at me with her astoundingly blue eyes. Up close, I could see that the net of scars on her hands and face were from age, not from fire. "We have come to guide you," she said.

I looked up at the bed where my mother was resting, sitting up and still unconscious. Supergirl was lying contentedly under one of my mother's arms, snuggled against her chest. The bulimic was lying curled the same way under the other arm. They all looked content, even my mother, who was snoring lightly.

"They are taking what they need," the burned girl said.

"What about you?"

"That's the trick," she said, and, without seeming to walk, she moved toward me.

In Peru Don Eduardo had told us to imagine a light inside our bellies, right behind our navels. It would feel as blinding as a piece of the sun, he said. I hadn't been able to understand what he meant. As the burned girl moved toward me, I did. She entered me somewhere near my navel, and I began to shudder from so much light.

When the nurse arrived, the children were gone, and I knew I would not see them again. *Unless you call us,* a voice whispered inside my head.

I was exhausted, but I asked the nurse if she would settle herself in the second bedroom and leave me alone to sit with my mother. "I know what to do. Just keep her sitting up and don't let her touch her face."

The nurse was a sallow, grim young woman who seemed relieved by my request. "I'll be close by."

All night I sat by my mother, who slept. Once I helped her to the bathroom, and twice I got her juice. I kept the TV on with the sound turned down, content to watch the blue glow and the flickering images. The nurse came in several times to check on us. "We're fine in here," I said.

After sunrise I slept a few hours. While I was sleeping, a

second nurse had replaced the first, and we chatted briefly about the hot weather.

Later in the morning, in the kitchen, I checked the expiration date on a box of cereal. It was okay. I poured myself a bowl, mixing it with juice, because I was wary of the milk.

After I ate, I called Meg and told her the visions were gone, it had been exactly the right thing to take care of my mother, and I'd try to explain when I got home. "You should *see* her. No telling what's been happening under those bandages."

"You do sound different, Ellen. I'm so glad."

"You," I said, "you sound wonderful."

When I went back to my mother's bedroom, she was awake. She asked me to bring her a hand mirror. "I can't remember a thing from last night," she said, staring at her bruised eyes and nose and mouth surrounded by the swaths of bandages. "My goodness, honey, I look dreadful. Look at those tubes. I look like a giant bug. What's happened? How did you get me home?"

"It was easy. Not much."

She looked away from herself and at me, and I saw myself reflected in her eyes. "You must be starving, Ellen Larraine. Did you get some breakfast?"

"I did," I said. "Anyway, I'm not hungry."

A Note on the Type

The text of this book was composed in a film version of Palatino, a typeface designed by the noted German typographer Hermann Zapf. Named after Giovanbattista Palatino, a writing master of Renaissance Italy, Palatino was the first of Zapf's typefaces to be introduced in America. The first designs for the face were made in 1948, and the fonts for the complete face were issued between 1950 and 1952. Like all Zapf-designed typefaces, Palatino is beautifully balanced and exceedingly readable.

Composed, printed, and bound by The Haddon Craftsmen, Inc.,
Scranton, Pennsylvania
Designed by Mia Vander Els